The Goat in the Garage

BOB LOGAN

For the real Doris

*Many thanks to all my family and friends
who helped me along this journey.*

CHAPTER ONE

2003

Gary could feel his heart pounding as he took aim. Steady now, he said to himself. It would be his last and only chance in this game of survival. Missing wasn't an option. He went through the protocol step by step: Firming his grip. Holding his breath. Visualizing the hit. Then he shot.

CRACK!

As usual, the cue ball seemed to have a mind of its own as it hit the eight ball just off center and proceeded to find the corner pocket. Scratch! Nicky, curled up nearby, gave a single wag of his tail and a doleful look at Gary, somehow knowing his master's lament.

"You know, Jo, this all started with that loose rack of yours!" said Gary.

"Leave my boobs out of this," replied Jo glancing down at her ample chest.

"Yeah, right. Next time rack 'em tight like you're supposed to."

"This game was all evened up until that last shot. You should have your eyes examined and while you're at it, do the rest of your head."

Gary's rec room was in the basement of his modest rancher located among a few dozen other middle-class

1

houses in the maturing development. He'd gotten the pool table for free from a guy he met while hanging out at a car restoration shop nearby. 'Just get it out of my house' was all Gary needed to hear. A couple of strong friends and a pickup truck got the heavy pool table back to Gary's house. It was a little rough around the edges but being handy, Gary decided to dismantle it and restore its former glory. His research showed it was built in the 1920s and must have been in a pool hall at that time as evidenced by the cigarette burns on the walnut rails. He could envision a smoke-filled room with a bunch of guys hanging out with ciggies in their hands, a deck of Luckies stuck in a T-shirt sleeve, and cold beers all around. Those dark burns would stay to maintain its character, and he bought new tan felt and matching chalk to finish the job. Nicky, his ever-faithful golden mutt, provided constant companionship during the weeks-long project and his wife, Doris, figured it would keep him out of the trouble that followed him like a shadow.

"One day I'll learn to hit a straight shot," Gary remarked.

"A lot of felt under that shot Gary. Sometimes those are the hardest."

"I've had this table for what, two years? You'd think I'd practice occasionally."

"You know how it goes. You get something and you're all excited at first but after a few weeks the blush is off the rose, and it just collects dust."

"That's an example of my short attention span. I gotta focus. When I have a project like this pool table it's like I'm on a mission. I have a goal. And the results speak for themselves."

"I couldn't agree more," said Jo. "You do good work when you put your mind to it."

"I wish I felt that way about my day job. Managing a shoe store ain't what I'd envisioned for a career."

"Quit," replied Jo.

"And do what? I have a mortgage, kids, the works. I'm stuck for a few more years."

"Then you need another outlet, another project."

"The only reason I got this pool table project was because it was free. A hundred bucks for materials wasn't a problem. The wifey would be hard on my case if I spent too much".

"You've been married thirty years. Haven't you learned how to handle Doris?" asked Jo, who usually knew the answer before she asked a question.

"Yes and no. Mostly no. How do you handle Fred."

"We have a system. I say 'yes'... he says 'yes'.

"Or else what?"

"He sleeps on the couch."

"That's cruel."

"It works though."

"I just thought of a birthday gift for your hubby."

"I think I feel a Garyism coming. Ok what?"

"A girlie magazine and a box of Kleenex!"

"You are one sick dude Gary Miller."

Jo lived just across the street and was a Jo-of-all-trades. She grew up connected at the hip with her dad, a tool and die maker who tinkered with cars after work. Apprenticed as his gofer at the age of five, she watched and learned and by sixteen was adept at tuning up a car and replacing brake pads. Her teenage boyfriends were just as enamored with her mechanical skills as they were with her petite, shapely figure, and pretty face. Her biggest laments were trying to keep the grease from under fingernails or scuffing her favorite red nail polish. Damn if she didn't have a skinned knuckle for the senior prom as a result of using an adjustable wrench when a properly sized box wrench was the right tool for the job. Lesson learned.

Early on she'd found the love of her life in Fred, an all-through-high-school classmate who favored reading over doing. Jo, Doris and next-door neighbor Maggie all loved to cook and met regularly in each other's kitchens to try new recipes or bake a cake that would always get accolades from the guys. And being the neighborhood mechanic, Jo's honey-do list usually included some task at a neighbor's house provided there was beer on hand or a plate full of cookies.

"So, Gary, wanna play best of eleven?" asked Jo.

"That means I gotta win six straight," said Gary as he twisted the chalk cube on his cue tip.

"I'm game providing you have enough beer in the fridge. By the way, I didn't see any more light beer, what gives?"

"Light and beer are oxymorons, and you must be a moron to drink one. Present company excluded."

"Tastes great and less filling!"

"Lies, all lies," said Gary. "Looks and tastes like camel piss if you ask me. I only drink beer that conforms to the German purity law… only water, barley malt and hops for the ingredients, and absolutely no ruining it by making it 'light'.".

"You buy St. Pauli Girl for the picture of the buxom fraulein on the box! Its conformity is a bonus."

"It's not a perfect world, Jo. Besides I'm a sucker for cleavage."

"Hey Gary, I just got a brilliant idea. I'll share it with you for another beer."

"Hmm. I didn't know your brain's rheostat went beyond dim. But you're a cheap date so... ok, shoot," said Gary.

"You've been talking about those old cars you used to drive. Why not buy a needy classic car and fix it up?

"I'll tell you why not... her name begins with a 'D'.

"Unbelievable. Are you a man or a mouse?"

Nicky's ears perked up at the word mouse, gave a heads up look around and seeing nothing, he gave his muzzle a quick lick and settled his head back down on his front paws.

"I refuse to answer on the grounds that my answer would tend to incinerate me. Squeak!"

"Look Mickey, I know you hate computers but listen up. Out there in cyberspace there are auctions for crashed cars, some of which are old classics. Why don't you check 'em out and maybe you can find a project. My dad used to fix up old cars all the time. It would be fun for me too. I could teach you how to do it."

"Yet another slight to my masculinity! I can change oil and top off a radiator to boot!"

"Yeah, yeah. I know you can. Such a thin skin. Let's get on the laptop, and I'll show you the site.

###

With Nicky at their heels, they climbed the stairs to the kitchen which was open to the dining and living rooms thanks to Gary having removed the walls years ago in a previous project. Gary and Doris shared a workspace which consisted of a Gary-restored drafting table and on its smooth wooden top sat an older Dell laptop that could barely handle a dated Windows 98. Reboot was the operative word, and Gary had little patience for it but buying a new one wasn't in the tight budget. Jo, on the other hand, knew its idiosyncrasies having searched recipes with Doris. It only took a minute for her to have it up and running. She typed 'Acme Auto Auctions' into the search engine.

"Gary look. This is it. Just type in whatever make of car you're looking for and it displays a list of what they currently have and the date of the auction for that particular car. If you don't find anything, check back occasionally to search again. Easy, peasy."

"Yeah, and pricey dicey I'll bet. Where do I get the money to buy this relic if I find one?"

"What about that little nest egg you told me about? The dough from your accident. Three grand or there-abouts, no?"

"Well, there is that. But I promised Doris, we'd save it for a rainy day and frankly there ain't much more than that in all our savings."

"When you made that promise you had your fingers crossed, right?"

"Of course."

"Well then, you're good to go. Now what would be the car of your dreams?"

"One like my dad owned when I was sixteen. A 1966 Pontiac GTO. I was the cat's patootie when I drove it around school."

"GTO, huh? I know the car but what does "GTO" stand for?" asked Jo.

"It's Italian for Gran Turismo Omologato. It means suited for grand touring racing. You soup up a production car and race it. I guess the guys at Pontiac borrowed the term."

Way back in 1966 when his dad was car shopping, Gary was constantly badgering him about getting a GTO. It was during those halcyon days of big American muscle cars and the GTO was one of the best. A big 389 cubic inch engine pumping out 335 horsepower. The '66 model was good looking too with vertical headlights, swept back tunnel roof and louvered taillights. The popular band 'Ronnie and the Daytonas' had a hit song in "Little GTO" which Gary still had on a 45 record. It took a while to convince dad and though he opted not to get the 'three duces and a four speed', choosing an automatic instead, their metallic green GTO was great looking and could beat most other cars in a drag race.

"You had all the girls wanting a ride, right?" asked Jo.

"Of course. But the guys loved it too being that I hung out with car nuts. Buried the needle one night at 120 mph. The car only had six hundred miles on it. Dumb."

"E pluribus unum. The first of many dumb things I've heard about ol' Gary," said Jo.

"Oh, and I beat a Comet Cyclone in a drag race. It had a 390 cubic inch motor and a 4-speed but I nosed him out at the finish. What a night!"

"Your old man never suspected?"

"Nope. But he might have wondered why the rear tires needed replacement so quickly. That Goat could really lay rubber!"

"Goat?"

Nicky cocked his head at that word as something in his canine brain sensed that a mission could be afoot akin to chasing rabbits and squirrels.

"Easy there Nickster," Gary said as he stooped over and petted Nicky. "Yeah, Goat," he continued. "Kind of a pronunciation of GTO... sort of."

"But hey Gary, your three grand ain't gonna get you far in this day and age. It's a new millenium man. Three large won't even buy you a good paint job."

"Don't bust my bubble. FYI, I hit the lotto for twenty-five bucks just last week. I'm on a roll!"

"Save that dough for a half tank of gas."

"Hey, stranger things have happened. Even a blind squirrel finds a nut now and then. Maybe no one else will show up for the auction. I'm feelin' lucky!"

"Luck favors the well-prepared, Gary."

"I'm prepped! I got the vision. That's all I need for now."

"And you got me in your corner! I'm with you all the way Gary. We'll do this!"

"Oh baby! You got me psyched! Thanks Jo. I feel like a new man. A man on a mission!"

CHAPTER TWO

1967

Gary was sixteen when his parents decided to buy a new car and he, being a bit of a motor head, decided to exert whatever influence in that decision that he could muster. This urging ranged from clipping ads out of the newspaper to putting on a glum face when put off by dad. His mom referred to this as 'hanging his snoot.' Well, Gary thought, whatever it takes.

He didn't know exactly why the quest for a new car had begun. Perhaps the '55 Dodge Royal Lancer that dad drove was using a bit too much oil or maybe he was having a mid-life crisis. Gary didn't much care and the hunt was on.

In the 1960s, guys were pretty much aligned with the cars that their parents drove. If dad drove a Ford Mustang, you were a Ford guy. If he drove a Chevelle, you were a GM guy. But Gary was an outlier being a GM guy when dad had that Dodge. This had much to do with his older brother buying a jet black '59 Chevy Impala coupe, a much more exciting vehicle than the old Dodge. They'd ridden to Reading, Pennsylvania with their dad to pick it up at the dealership. On the way home, with Gary in the back, they stopped at the Tropical Treat to get some food. They pulled in and took an ordering space and asked for two Cokes and one chocolate milkshake which were promptly delivered by a cute and shapely carhop.

Handing the shake back to Gary, his brother admonished him to not spill it. Gary grabbed the shake and as he sat back in the seat, he squeezed the large paper cup a little too hard and emptied half of the contents on himself and the seat. Were it not for dad, Gary truly believed that his short life would have ended right there.

That Impala's glossy black body was contrasted with a bright red interior and under the hood was a powerful 348 cubic inch V8 motor. You could bury the needle on a straightaway if you had enough cajónes and if the car's rear end didn't become airborne due to the flat 'wings' designed into the body. Those wings were a 90 degree turn from the 'fins' featured on many cars of the 1950s. By 1961, though, both the fins and wings were purged from the stylists' drawing boards and tastes turned to a more streamlined contour and even larger engines. Hence the GTO.

GM's John Delorean was responsible for putting the big motor under the hood of the demure Pontiac Tempest. A hood scoop and "GTO" badging were not-so-subtle hints of the immense power that laid within. Uniquely, the badging also proclaimed a '6.5 LITRE' engine, perhaps a hat tip to a concocted European legacy where none existed. Now what was the formula for converting litres to cubic inches?

To Gary, this was the car that should grace the home driveway and be the envy of his friends and a probable girl magnet as well. The lobbying from Gary was incessant and he finally convinced his parents to at least take a look at a GTO at the local dealership. Well, that magic worked and seeing that beautiful metallic green car on the showroom floor, dad and mom were taken hook, line and sinker. They finagled the $3200 sticker price somehow, and Gary's mission was accomplished. Wait until the guys hear about this!

Alone in a new GTO at sixteen was once beyond his comprehension but here he was behind the wheel and wanting to share the moment with a friend. Jack, his motorhead buddy, was the first to take a ride in the GTO.

"Gary, this car is so cool. I can't believe you talked your parents into buying it. Have they lost their minds?"

"I don't think that dad realizes its stature as a muscle car. To him, it's just new wheels with a little more umph."

"335 umphs if I remember correctly," said Jack. "That's about twice the power of what the Dodge had."

"Well, let's keep that a secret. But I've got to keep this beautiful beast on a leash for a while yet. It needs to get broken in."

"How so?"

"The owner's manual says that for the first six hundred miles you must keep the speed down so that the engine's internal parts find their own grove so to speak. The pistons, rings, and cylinder walls need to get to know one another slowly. It's better for the car in the long run."

"So, what happens after six hundred miles?"

"We take it up on Route 100 and bury the needle," Gary announced. "That's a hundred and twenty miles per hour on the speedometer. I've never been that fast."

"Yeah, baby. That's what I'm talkin' about! How many more miles until the break- in period is over?"

"One hundred fifty-five. It'll be a few more days yet. Maybe by the weekend."

"No rain in the forecast. Can you get it Saturday night?"

"Yeah. My aunt and uncle will be visiting and taking

my parents to the Italian club for pizza so the car will be home. I can pick you up around eight o'clock if you're up for it."

"Sure am. But ask your mom to bring some of that pizza home. It's the best."

By Saturday, the GTO had six hundred and eighty miles on it, well beyond the break in range and Gary figured it should be time to rock and roll. He picked up Jack as they had planned and headed directly for the mile-long straightaway on Route 100 between Pottstown and Boyertown. It was a divided highway, two lanes in each direction with a wide grassy strip separating northbound from southbound. Now if they could just avoid any traffic.

"Jack, keep your head on a swivel and let me know if you see any cops. They patrol this stretch on the rare occasion that they're not eating donuts at the diner."

"I just saw a patrol car headed south. We should be good to go heading north."

"We're about a mile away from the long straight section, and no cars in the way so far. Seat belts buckled. I think we're ready."

The straightaway came into view as they motored along at fifty miles an hour. Gary's hands gripped the steering wheel a little harder and his blood pressure rose a little higher. Seeing no traffic ahead and nothing in the rearview mirror, he pressed his right foot to the floor. The GTO automatically downshifted, and the RPMs instantly surged as the guys were pressed back into their seats. The GTO literally leapt forward for all its worth then upshifted into high gear.

"Holy cannoli! This car can move!" Jack shouted over the roaring engine.

"Eighty… Ninety… One hundred…!" exclaimed Gary as he glanced at the speedometer while keeping the car straddling both northbound lanes.

"You can do it Gary. Pedal to the metal!"

"Not much straight road left. One hundred ten…" Gary exclaimed as the dashed lines on the roadway slipped under the car at an astonishing rate. 'Mabelene' would have been the perfect song to accompany this wild escapade with Chuck Berry singing 'a hundred and ten a halfa mile ahead.'

"Go man go!"

"There! One twenty on the button! Oh baby!" Gary shouted as he finally let up on the gas.

The arrow-straight highway ended as they approached a slight hill after which it curved gently to the left just before the exit to Boyertown. Gary tapped the brakes. Uh Oh… There was a rattling shutter as the brake pads bounced off the drums, not wanting to engage properly. They crested the hill at ninety miles per hour and Gary eased the GTO into the quickly approaching left bend. He tried the brakes again and this time they held. They slowed to sixty and Gary took the exit while hard on the brakes. At the traffic light, they collected their thoughts.

"What was that weird rumbling all about?" gasped Jack. "It freaked me out."

"Beats me," replied Gary. "I guess the brakes don't like stopping from that speed. Maybe they're too new."

"Let's not do that again. I don't think my sphincter muscles can take it."

"I heard you fart. You'll have to disinfect the seat later."

13

"I hope my underwear is still white."

"Don't even go there. Just be happy that we hit the target and lived to talk about it."

"May I suggest we keep it to ourselves and not tell anyone lest your dad find out."

"You know, Jack. Once in a while, a long while, you come up with a good idea."

"I'll take that as a compliment although it was reluctantly given."

"I give credit where credit is due. Speaking of credit, you still owe me two bucks for the Girl Scout cookies courtesy of my little cousin."

"But you ate half of them!"

"And thank you for sharing. I'll pull into a gas station, and you can pay."

"I guess I'm getting off cheap. That thrill ride tonight was worth every penny," admitted Jack. "And if you survive into adulthood, you can tell your children all about it."

"Children? I don't even have a girlfriend yet."

"Maybe. But if you did, her name would probably start with a 'D'."

Gary puzzled in thought for a moment. Ohh, her! Gary smiled, turned the GTO left and headed for home.

CHAPTER THREE

To prime the pump, Jo suggested that they go to a big regional car show in Carlisle PA which was specifically themed to feature classic American Iron… big old cars most of which had giant engines. They were known as 'muscle' cars and were produced by all the major US car companies which constantly tried to outdo each other. More cubic inches, more horsepower, and slick styling with badges that denoted big power under the hood were the norm…"427" or "396" were ubiquitous. A big engine came with bragging rights and an inflated ego. Some racers even dropped these big block engines into British cars like the famous Ford Cobra, the Cadillac-powered Allard, or the Sunbeam Tiger. Winning at a speedway or quarter mile drag strip got more attention and sold more cars. Lots more. And the more horsepower and options that you ordered for your car, the more profits for the manufacturers. But most guys didn't care. They were in it for speed and sex. After all, what young lady of the '60s didn't want a ride in a fancy car with a guy amped up on testosterone?

Gary hadn't been to a car show in years, and decided what the heck, he'd go. On the day of the show, Jo picked him up in her new 2003 BMW Z4 and headed west on the Pennsylvania Turnpike. When they got there, it didn't take long for him to be drooling over each and every car.

He'd seen 'em all back in the day and here they were again in prime condition. And when they finally found a corral of GTO's, Gary was in heaven.

"Jo, look at this one! You can eat off the engine it's so clean. Like it was built yesterday."

"I just knew you'd love this show. All these cars are fantastic."

"Every inch of this GTO brings back memories. The dashboard layout, the pleated seats, and of course the 389 engines. Every time I washed my dad's car, I'd make sure the chrome valve covers shined along with the rest of the engine compartment. Exactly like this one."

The owners of the cars were milling about or sitting on folding camp chairs near their cars. Gary caught one guy's eye and walked over to him.

"Yours?" Gary asked sheepishly to an older gentleman with a GTO logo on his baseball cap.

"Yeah," the man replied.

"My dad had one but in metallic green with a black interior. Lots of good memories. Have you owned it long?"

"A few years. The restoration took a while."

"You do good work though. So nice. I'm thinking of buying one to restore myself."

"Funny… You don't come across as a complete idiot."

"He's working on his doctorate in idiotology as we speak. Just ask his wife," Jo chided.

"I know. I know," said Gary. "It's a labor of love."

"That's an understatement," replied the man. "Love, time, more money, more time… did I mention money?"

"Therein lies the problem. I've got precious little of each," said Gary. "That said, I'd like to find one to work on and maybe someday have one that looks as good as yours."

"Well, more power to you. Obviously, I've been

there, done that. I didn't have much money either when I started down this path but it kinda gets into your blood. Go for it, my friend."

"A lot of bucks invested in this car?" asked Jo.

"No comment," replied the man.

"That much huh?"

The man winked and grinned as he looked over at his wife who frowned in uncertain approval.

"Hey, you can't take it with you," he continued, "so you might as well enjoy what you got, while you got it. But the car is only part of the bargain. You get to meet a lot of great people to hang out with, to go to car shows, to go on road trips to wherever. It's a whole package. I hope you find your dream."

"Yeah, thanks. This has been a great inspiration," said Gary as he waved so long.

"Well, Gary. Are you psyched up about a project yet?" asked Jo.

"I'm out of my mind psyched. Let's check out the rest of these Goats and then hit the car parts section."

"We can ask around and maybe somebody will have a lead on a project car."

"I'm guessing that these shows get a lot of guys looking for projects. We might have to let things cool down for a bit."

"Gary, you gotta strike while the iron's hot. Find the right car at a good price and buy it, no haggling."

"I was born to haggle, Jo. Hell, I'm a hagglin' fool."

"Agreed on the fool part."

"You would."

"Hey, look, there's a kiosk for Acme Auto Auctions. That's the one I told you about. Let's go check it out."

As they sauntered over, they passed an apparel stand

and at Jo's urging, Gary stopped to buy a baseball cap emblazoned with a GTO logo, exactly like the one the old guy was wearing. This insignificant purchase was the first step, albeit small, in getting Gary to start opening his wallet toward the goal of getting a project car. With it, the die was cast.

"Looks great on you Gary," said Jo. "Puts you in the right frame of mind."

"Yeah, I like it," said Gary as he looked in the mirror hanging on the hat rack and crimped the brim a bit narrower. "But I gotta keep this outta sight at home lest Doris get wind of our plot."

"Good thinkin'. Can't put the car before the horsepower… or something like that."

When they got to the auction kiosk, they picked up a brochure that explained their services. The gal behind the table gave them each a nice bottle cozy and a key chain printed with their website address.

"Ever use our auctions?" she asked.

"No, not yet. But I might start looking for a project car."

"Let me guess… hmmm… GTO?"

"Wow, how'd you guess?" asked Gary.

She pointed to Gary's new hat and tapped her forehead.

"He's got short term memory problems, measured in milliseconds," Jo said.

"Oh, yeah, the hat," remembered Gary.

"I'm sure you'll find what you're looking for on our site. Sooner or later. And we have delivery services too. Just call us if you have any questions."

"His sanity is in question. Any advice for that?" asked Jo.

"Hmm, that's out of my lane. Try the beer kiosk. Maybe he'll come around after a few brews."

They thanked her for the timely suggestion since their stomachs were growling and the afternoon heat had them feeling a bit dehydrated. They ambled over to the food court, and Gary grabbed a beer and a hotdog with kraut and mustard, and a plain dog and diet Coke for Jo.

"How can you and Doris eat just plain hot dogs? Have you no gastronomical etiquette?"

"I, for one, am a minimalist. It's what I do."

Gary proffered a toast to GTOs and took three swallows of cold beer right off the top.

"Ahhh, that hits the spot."

"Do you know the record for eating hot dogs?"

"Yep. Seventy-six dogs and buns. But that guy ain't drinkin'....," Gary stops to burp, "... beer."

"Correctamundo. Heck, I'm full after one dog and one soda."

"It must take him three days to digest all that. Wouldn't want to be him the morning after," said Gary.

"I'd say something sophomoric and crude but I'm on the grown-up wagon," said Jo.

"A tiger can't change its stripes."

"I'm testing my willpower. Speaking of power, let's check out the rest of these muscle cars."

After three more hours of ogling GTOs, Corvettes, Cobras, Mustangs and miscellaneous hemi-powered Chrysler cars, they were foot weary but emotionally pumped. They worked their way back toward Jo's car through the used parts lanes to get a feel for availability should the need arise. They collected business cards and phone numbers from the GM guys and were assured that they could get any part for a '66 Goat.

Back at the car Gary offered to drive.

"Thanks, but you been drinkin'," said Jo.

"That was three hours ago and only one beer. And I sweated that one out by two o'clock."

"Tell it to the judge. Naw, this day is on me. So, what's your prognosis on the project?"

"I'm in. All in. That is, of course, if I find a GTO that I can afford. And keep this a secret from you know who."

"Never hear of her," said Jo. And pursing her lips whispers, "muy wips ahh sweeled."

"Good. If the cat gets out of the bag, she'll put the kibosh on my dreams."

Jo pulled out of the vast parking lot and headed east on Rt. 11 having decided to take the scenic route back. About a half hour into the ride, Gary's hunger returned.

"Hey, let's stop to get some ice cream," said Gary. "I'm getting hungry again, and we're due for a treat."

"Ok. I'm sure there's a Dairy Queen around here somewhere."

"A DQ? Are you insane?

"Yes, to your first question. And 'not certifiably' to your second."

"We are in Amish, Mennonite, and Pennsylvania Dutch country. Here we have 'creameries.' We got hand-made ice cream in dozens of flavors. Does DQ have that?"

"I want soft serve vanilla… with chopped peanuts," said Jo.

"You can bring a horse to water…"

"I know, I know. Hey, up ahead there. It's one of your creameries. And the sign says soft serve too!"

"Looks like we hit the bifecta. Pull in."

Jo pulled into the parking lot of Ziggenfuss's ice cream parlor. They got out and strode up to the order window. Gary got a double dip butter pecan and Jo her vanilla softie with chopped peanuts. As they licked away, Gary noticed that they had a bake shop inside.

"I'm gonna get something sweet for the spouses. I'll only be a minute."

"Ok," said Jo. "I'll wait in the car with the A/C on full blast to keep this ice cream from melting."

Gary went inside and found a trove of Dutch-baked goodies. There was an elderly lady, plainly dressed with her gray hair in a bun. She stood smiling behind the glass display counter which was filled with big donuts, cupcakes, Danishes, and sticky buns.

"Hi," said Gary. "My wife loves sticky buns. I'll take a half-dozen pack."

"Male or female?" asked the lady.

"Huh? What's the difference?" asked Gary as he took a bite of his big cone.

"The males have nuts," the lady deadpanned.

Gary coughed up the swallow of ice cream and a pecan piece got caught in his throat. He stifled a laugh to stop himself from spitting the ice cream all over the glass display case.

"Oh, sorry. Was it something I said?" the lady chuckled.

"I'll bet you say that to all the guys. I'll have the males," Gary sputtered.

She wrapped up the big, doughy gooey pastries and handed the bag to Gary. He bid the lady good day, went out the door and jumped into the waiting car with Jo. Then they headed down the road, still enjoying their ice cream cones.

Jo was a little distracted as she drove. She was licking the melting ice cream and trying to keep the peanut pieces from falling onto her lap. She took one big circular lick, and the car edged onto the stoney berm.

"Jo! Pay attention. You're running off the road."

"Do you know how hard it is to drive while licking your nuts?" Jo innocently proffered.

This time Gary couldn't contain this mouthful of butter pecan as he spit it all over the dashboard. The top scoop fell off and landed in his crotch. Jo finally realized what she'd said and had to pull off the road as tears of laughter filled her eyes. Gary grabbed the loose scoop and plopped it back atop his cone. They laughed for five minutes before normal conversation could resume.

"Oh baby, Jo. That was the funniest thing you ever said."

"No malice aforethought. It just popped out."

"And to answer your question… No, I don't know how hard it is to lick one's nuts, and by the way, how would you know?

"Educated guess… I guess. I'm a Tom boy if you hadn't noticed."

"Wouldn't have it any other way. Let's get back on the road. Assuming your nuts are in order."

"Lickin' as we speak."

Jo put the car in gear, and Gary turned up the radio. He'd have some 'splainin' to do about the ice cream stains on his pants.

Jo had just finished her cone when they pulled up to a stop light outside of Camp Hill. Her little BMW Z4 was a quick machine, and she had a bit of a heavy foot especially if someone challenged her. She and Fred bought it new as her birthday present and only drove it on sunny days or special occasions like today. She was happy that she opted for the "M" model with a higher horsepower engine. The six-speed manual gearbox suited her to a T.

While waiting for the light to change, a pair of guys in a rather loud vintage Dodge Charger pulled up beside them. Gary glanced over and smiled.

"Jo, those guys wanna race," said Gary.

"Yeah? What make you think that?"

The driver of the Charger gunned his engine twice.

"Does that answer your question?"

Just then the light turned green, and the Charger squealed its tires as it lunged forward. Jo's mind switched into its primal competitive mode which instantly responded by instructing her right foot to depress the gas pedal… all the way. The Charger was already a car length in front as she hit the gas. The Z4's traction control prohibited tire spin, and it caught up with the Charger whose wheels finally stopped smoking. Hitting second gear, Jo had 'em by a half car length and was pulling away as the BMW entered its sweet torque range up around 5500 rpm.

"Jo, slow the hell down. The speed limit is 45 and your doin' sixty and climbing!"

"Beat those hombres, didn't I?" said Jo as she let off the gas. "Those 340 ponies under the hood ain't shy."

The Charger zipped by still accelerating, and its passenger gave a thumbs up as they turned off onto an expressway ramp.

"Yeah, you beat 'em," said Gary as he glanced over his shoulder. "But I doubt that cop is going to present you with a trophy."

"What cop?" asked Jo as she looked around then glanced at her rearview mirror. "Oh, that cop."

The light bar on the copmobile was flashing and two chirps on the siren was all it took to convince Jo to pull over.

23

"Dang, I've been so good for so long. I can't believe I'm getting pulled over."

"Jo, I'm going to shout, 'She's got weed!' when the cop walks up."

"Do that Gary and I'll kill you. Just sit there and shut up."

"I'll try."

The local municipal cop pulled up behind the BMW and did her license check thing. She then walked up to the BMW and motioned to roll down the window.

"Hi Officer Jones," said Jo as she read her lapel nametag. "Beautiful day, isn't it?"

"Yes, lovely day. Might I see your driver's license and owner's card please?" she asked.

"Why of course. Here they are. By the way, you have a lovely color on your nails."

"Thank you. I'm trying to compliment the blue uniform. So, if I might ask, did you happen to see the speed limit sign as you were zipping through my town here?"

"Why yes, I did. Forty-five if I'm not mistaken," Jo answered.

"Quite right. However, you seemed to have exceeded that limit just as you shifted gears which I heard you do as you pulled away from the Charger."

"Well, I do admit that I may have gotten carried away a bit. But what about that Charger?"

"My associates on the expressway are enlightening him as we speak."

"Ahh, good, very efficient. And you have my assurance that I am also enlightened," remarked Jo.

Gary had been stifling a laugh as this discourse went on. Jo banged her fist into his leg to get him to stop.

"Who's your compatriot?" asked the officer.

"Just some idiot neighbor of mine."

"Where are you two headed?"

"Home, near Reading. We were at the car show in Carlisle."

The officer bent over to look in at Gary and smiled. Gary waved and smiled back.

"Hi, Officer Jones. Nice to make your acquaintance," said Gary.

"Just so you two know, drag racing down Main Street is frowned upon."

"Hey, but the speed limit doesn't say anything about how quickly you attain the limit, does it?" questioned Gary.

"Jesus, Gary, can't you for once just sit there and shut the hell up?" said Jo. "I don't need no points."

"I see by your hat that you have a GTO," the officer said to Gary.

"I wish I had. I'm trying to find one to restore. Jo here is helping me. I bought the hat at Carlisle from a lady named Marge at the apparel kiosk."

"Marge happens to be my aunt," said Officer Jones. "Her husband has a GTO. Our family goes way back on Goats."

"You don't say! Small world, isn't it?" said Gary.

"Well, I checked your background, and you have no priors and no points," said the officer as she handed Jo back her cards. "Let's just say that today didn't happen. That is if you promise to behave."

"I will, I promise. The Charger kinda got my goat so to speak," said Jo.

Officer Jones smiled and walked back to her cruiser, and Jo breathed a sigh of relief.

"Boy that was close. If it wasn't for my GTO hat, you'd have gotten a ticket for sure," Gary said.

"Yeah, I'm glad I urged you to buy it. By the way, let's keep this little incident on a need-to-know basis with Fred. As in he doesn't need to know. He gets concerned when I go for a drive in this car... my lead foot has a reputation."

"Your name and number are found on a stall in the men's room at Maple Grove Dragway. It says, 'for a good race, call Jo at 610-223-eat my dust!'"

"So that's where all the crank calls were coming from."

"Serves you right. You're a Don Garlits wannabe."

"Gosh no. This baby is as much as I need, more than enough actually."

"What's that? One never has enough horsepower."

"Oh yeah? Let's switch. You drive the rest of the way home and see if you can avoid getting a ticket."

"You're gonna let me drive your pride and joy? You only let Fred drive it once."

"Once too often if you ask me. He ground the gears shifting from second to third. Then again at third to fourth. I had him pull over before the tranny fell out."

"You gotta thin skin. I promise not to grind you a pound. And no tickets either. I know what I'm doing."

Gary may have spoken too soon. He was already a little stiff from walking around the car show and sitting still in the BMW tightened up what seemed to him like most of his muscles. The low-slung BMW was like a deep hammock and extricating himself was a chore accompanied by groans and mumbled oaths.

"I'm gonna buy you a set of spring spacers to jack up this car a foot," said Gary as he stretched his back. "Thankfully a GTO ain't this low."

26

"Weren't you doing yoga and quid pro quo?" asked Jo. "Don't they help?"

"It's called qigong, and evidently it has yet to take full effect."

Gary struggled into the driver's seat and with some contortions, got his longish legs into the foot well.

"You shoudda put the seat all the way back," commented Jo.

"Now you tell me," reflected Gary as he pressed the seat control and moved it back a few inches. "I thought you were taller."

"Only when I wear high-heeled sneakers," responded Jo. "Which reminds me to get some oldies going on the radio."

As Jo scanned the airwaves, Gary adjusted the mirrors, got himself generally settled in and cranked up the engine. He goosed the throttle a few times, the sound of which brought a thin smile to his lips. This baby's got some moxie he thought as he selected first gear and slowly eased the clutch. He pulled out onto the roadway and immediately floored it. Jo's head slammed into the headrest as the BMW lurched forward.

"Geepers Gary, I've barely got my seatbelt on. Ease up a bit."

The speed limit came and went as Gary hit second gear and his right foot jammed the pedal. The Z4's engine quickly sought the red line as G forces pushed them deeply back into their seats. Having gotten that out of his system, he eased off the gas and coasted the speed back down.

"You know that the GTO has about the same horsepower as this BMW, but in a heavier package. We'll have to go to the dragway for a match race. As much as I love the Goats, I think this Bimmer would win hands down," lamented Gary.

27

"Fifty years of technology can make a big difference," said Jo. "They can really squeeze power out of engines nowadays and, just as importantly, get it to the ground without all the wheel spin."

"Yeah, that Charger back there couldn't rein in all those horses. I had the same problem with my dad's Goat. We used to drift backwards a bit then jam it into drive and floor it. I could lay a patch with both tires for a hundred feet… posi-traction be damned."

"Cheap thrills. I love the smell of smokin' tires in the morning!" added Jo.

Two chirps on the siren alerted Gary to check his rearview mirror and Jo to turn and look out the back only to see the flashing crossbar of the cruiser.

"She looks familiar, Gary. Un-be-lieve-a-ble. Methinks you are blued, screwed, and tattooed."

"Son of a sea witch," Gary mumbled as he pulled over.

Officer Jones took no time to run the plates having already done that a few minutes previously. She didn't look too happy as Gary watched her exit the cruiser and approach the BMW.

"Why, Officer Jones, so nice to see you again, I think," said Gary as she stood next to the car with her hands on her hips and shaking her head.

"Same car, but a different driver I see," said the officer. "Perhaps you didn't understand the agreement I thought I had clearly articulated not several minutes ago."

"Well, yes, I did understand but this is my first time driving this car. It kinda got away from me. It wants to go… quickly… forward."

"I was just about to have lunch, had turned the cruiser around, and out of the blue I hear the scream of a BMW's engine hitting 6000 rpms. It's a unique sound.

28

So, I put one and one together, turned around, and here we are getting reacquainted."

"And now you have the hangries to boot," suggested Gary. "I'm toast."

"Expensive toast I might add as I'm fresh out of warnings. Your comrade there got the last one of the day. That said, I do have some compassion. I'll allow you to choose your poison… fifteen over the limit or careless driving."

"Well, I was being very careful… really. So, I guess I'll take the fifteen over," said Gary.

"The better choice if I might add, though each award you three points."

"Been a while since I been awarded anything. Somehow, I don't feel too good about it."

"As you shouldn't. Hang tight while I write up your certificate of achievement," quipped the officer.

As she ambled back to the cruiser, Jo, who had been quiet as a mouse, let out a somewhat muffled laugh.

"I'm in the throes of agony here and you're laughing," said Gary.

"Can't… help… it. That 'award' bit was too funny.

"Luckily, I don't have any other points. I'll have to be good for a while until they clear my record. I'll need my driver's license whenever I get a GTO."

"That's the spirit, ace. Keep your thoughts focused on the goal… or goat as it were."

Officer Jones came back and handed Gary the ticket. She asked for his autograph to acknowledge his receipt, to which he complied.

"Thank you and good luck finding a GTO," the officer said. "My town ends about two blocks ahead. As nice as it was to meet you, see if you can keep it under the limit while in my realm. I'd hate to have to cuff and book a fellow GTO afficionado."

"I've learned my lesson, Officer Jones. I'll be a good boy," said Gary as he placed the ticket on the console and gave Officer Jones a brief wave goodbye.

Gary started up the BMW again and eased out onto the roadway and counted off the two blocks the cop had mentioned. As he passed the final traffic light his foot pressed down on the gas pedal.

"GARY!!!" said Jo excitedly.

Gary eased off the gas and said, "Just joshin' with you Jo. I'm cool."

Up ahead a road sign indicated the entrance to the PA turnpike and Gary flicked on the blinker. He pulled up to the booth and pulled out a paper ticket, handing it over to Jo.

"Let me tell you a story I heard about a friend of a friend way back when," said Gary.

"I'm all ears," answered Jo.

"So, my friend is a passenger in this guy's hot car and they're on the turnpike heading wherever. They get to their exit and the guy pulls up to the toll booth to ostensibly pay the tollkeeper."

"Ostensibly?" Jo questions.

"Yeah, hold on, you'll love this. So, the guy pulls up, and the tollkeeper asks for the ticket. The guy takes a marker and prints AMF in big letters on the ticket and hands it over to the tollkeeper. The tollkeeper looks at the ticket and asks, 'What's this AMF?' The guy puts the gear shift into first, turns to the tollkeeper and yells 'Arrivederci Motherflubber!' and peels out from the tollbooth in a cloud of burning rubber!"

"No way!" says Jo.

"Yes way," replies Gary. "My friend swore it happened and I believed him."

"But flubber? Who says that?"

"I do now that I'm trying to clean up my act. The original term would be too harsh for your virgin ears."

"FYI, very few parts of this body haven't been deflowered."

"None the less, it's a great story."

"Agreed, but don't get no ideas like that when we get off or I'll clobber you."

"As long as you're paying the toll, no need to."

"I'm starting to connect the dots. You're a chip off the old block in many ways."

"I suppose so especially when you consider the similarities in the company we keep."

"I'll take that as a compliment. AMF, huh? I envy that guy's creativity in discourse."

The turnpike ride was uneventful as Gary kept it near, but above, the speed limit only to juice it once when passing a Porsche. As they exited and pulled up to the tollbooth, Gary glanced at Jo who gave him the evil eye.

"What?" asked Gary.

"You know what," answered Jo.

"You're somethin'. You have no faith in humanity," said Gary shaking his head dejectedly.

Gary handed the ticket to this tollkeeper, a nice young lady with a welcoming smile.

"Beautiful day," Gary proffered to the lady.

"Yes, it is," she replied. "That'll be five fifty for the toll, please."

"Five fifty? Why that's an AMF ticket," said Gary.

Jo immediately became apoplectic and reached across Gary and thrust a ten spot out the window to the tollkeeper.

31

"Here ya go, keep the change," said Jo as her other hand depressed on Gary's crotch yielding a wide-eyed expression of submission on Gary's face.

"I have to give you the change," the lady explained. "Here ya go and please drive safely."

Jo got situated back on her side shaking her head.

"I wasn't gonna do nothin'," said Gary.

"Just makin' sure. I knew you'd get the message."

"I'm gonna tell Fred you assaulted me."

"No, *I'm* gonna tell Fred. He'll laugh his head off."

"Hmmm. Probably right. Ok, let's fuhgeddaboudit."

"Forget what?"

"No idea."

CHAPTER FOUR

While his parents were out doing the Friday evening shopping at the farmer's market in Gilbertsville, Gary was on the phone with Jack trying to set up a challenge race with another guy whose parents also had a big-motored coupe... a Mercury Cyclone GT that had a 390 cubic inch V8 putting out 335 hp... pretty much dead equal to the GTO. But this Cyclone had a four-speed manual tranny which would be an interesting match to the Goat's automatic. Now if only Gary could convince his dad to let him have the car tonight.

"So, Dale can get his dad's car and is up for a drag race," said Jack on the phone. "We can meet him later."

"My parents should be home soon. I'll tell them that I just wanna go down to Hilltop to meet my friends and get a burger and a shake. That shouldn't be a problem," replied Gary.

"I hope not, Gary. We've been talkin' up the Goat for weeks now, and Dale's been touting his prowess as a driver. That alone makes me wanna puke. We need to bring him down a peg or two."

"He's been drivin' that car around quite a bit and probably has the shifting down pat. Whether he can keep it together during a race is a different story though, Jack. His nerves might be his undoing."

"Don't count on that, Gary. Dale is a cool customer

if you ask me. I saw him go through the gears over on Route 422. Flat out peddle to the metal and he didn't miss a shift. Laid a patch of rubber from a dead stop and when he hit second gear, he was gone."

"Amateur. Laying rubber doesn't get you down the road. Feels good to do it. And sounds good too. It even smells good in a macho way if you like acrid smoke polluting the atmosphere, not to mention your lungs. But anyone can lay a patch. What you need to do is control the horsepower, so you just don't sit there and spin. I hope he does that when we race."

"Amateur? Like you are a big time drag racer? Don't get too far ahead of yourself lest you have your come-uppance.

"Hey, I took notes the last time we were over at Maple Grove Dragway. All the winning drivers barely left any rubber and only chirped the rear tires as they left the starting line. And that's what I plan to do."

"Sure. Until the adrenaline hits your brain and commands your right foot to jam the gas pedal into the floor," admonished Jack.

"Yeah, well, maybe. We'll both be amped up, so we'd be even in that aspect from the start. Hey, my parents just pulled in the driveway. Let's meet at Hilltop at nine o'clock."

"OK, Gary. Be there or be square. I'll let Dale know," said Jack as he disconnected.

Gary hadn't used the car for a couple of days, so it was easy to get his dad's okay as long as he put gas in it and stayed out of trouble. Well, he would put gas in it for sure. The trouble part was somewhat nebulous at this point.

Gary jumped in the Goat around eight o'clock and headed over to pick up Jack who lived about a mile from the Hilltop restaurant. But first, they needed to get the gas that Gary had promised his dad.

"Gary, head over to the Sunoco station on east High Street," said Jack.

"But gas is cheaper over at the Mobil station," replied Gary.

"Tonight, we'll need all the horsepower we can squeeze out of the motor. We need Sunoco 260, the highest octane available. Mobil won't cut it."

"Yeah, you're right. I can't be a cheapo when my reputation is on the line."

"I've arranged the stakes. We meet up again after the race and the loser buys burgers, fries and a Coke."

"I wanna milkshake, not a flippin' Coke."

"Well, arm wrestle him for the upgrade. That is assuming you win."

"Win? Of course I'll win. And you'll be right there beside me with your butt buckled into a bucket seat. I'm happy to share my glory."

"Gary, that is soooo magnanimous of you. Just be sure my butt is ahead of his butt at the finish."

Gary noticed a patrol car behind him as he put on his blinker and made a right into the brightly lit Sunoco station. The cop followed him in and pulled up on the opposite side of the gas pumps. Gary wondered if the cop was reading his mind and knew of the illegal mission that he was going to embark on later that night. The gas attendant walked up as Gary rolled down the window.

"Two bucks, 260. The gas cap is under the license plate," Gary said to the younger attendant.

"Gotcha. Nice GTO. Does it go fast?" asked the kid.

"Yeah, but not so loud. I don't want that cop to know," answered Gary.

35

"Oh, he knows! He knows!" chuckled Jack as he flashed a shy wave to the officer who nodded with a knowing smile.

The officer was, in fact, Chief Harvey Kline who was the only full-time cop in the township and everyone knew him. And the young'uns, especially the guys, feared him and gave him the respect he deserved. Perhaps it was the fear that made Gary's heart skip a beat as the Chief rolled down his window.

"Nice night for a joy ride. Isn't that dad's new car?" asked the Chief.

"Y-yeah," stammered Gary between heart skips.

"I see you're getting 260. Don't it take regular grade gas?"

"Uh, I think dad thinks it runs better with higher octane so that's what I get."

"It probably does," said the Chief. "I get 260 for this cruiser too. Don't want the criminals to outrun me."

The Chief's patrol car was a sedate looking four door Plymouth sedan. It was chalk white with a glossy black roof and gray cloth interior, and it looked like something your grandpa would drive or maybe that engineer geek that taught part-time at the high school. Aside from the red "bubble gum" dome light on the roof and the township crest painted on the door, it was a plain Jane car. The perfect sleeper… a vanilla car but with a Death by Chocolate motor under the hood.

The Chief had lobbied hard for this car, and he'd ordered the biggest motor Chrysler Corporation built. With 426 cubic inch displacement and a whopping 425 horsepower, the primal rumble it made at idle was the only clue that something special lurked beneath the hood. It was said that you could watch the fuel gauge drop when you floored it. The two big four-barrel carbs sucked gas like no tomorrow. Hey, if the township could afford the car, it could afford the gas.

"I heard you chased down a Corvette a few weeks ago," proffered Gary.

"Yeah, he thought he was fast, but I was faster," said the Chief. "Fortunately, he came to his senses and pulled over. For that dose of common sense, I just gave him a speeding ticket and not the evading arrest offense that I originally had in mind."

The attendant walked back up to Gary's window and took the two bucks.

"Have a nice night, big spender," quipped the kid.

"You too," said Gary who noticeably winced at the irony of the cheap purchase while driving a nice new car.

The two bucks did, however, buy about five gallons of gas which was enough to fuel the impending race and to satisfy one of dad's admonitions.

"Well, have a nice, safe evening," commanded the Chief. "And keep a leash on that beast."

"Yes, sir," was all Gary could say.

Jack was saying nothing. Just a sittin' and a grinnin'. Gary gave him a look that almost made Jack explode in laughter but somehow, he choked it back. Gary rolled up the window, turned the key and nudged the Goat out onto the street.

"That was close," said Gary. "And you didn't help with your ignorant behavior."

"Me? I didn't do nothin'," said Jack. "It's your face that had guilt written all over it. And you aren't even guilty… yet."

They headed east on High Street and on out to Sanatoga. Hilltop was a fixture on that side of town and marked the eastern end of the cruise circuit whose western terminus was the Tropical Treat Drive-In Restaurant, way over in Stowe. Pottstown was sandwiched in between where most of the evening action took place.

Hilltop's huge sign out front prominently mentioned "HAMBURGERS" as the main fare and hinted at a beverage to wash it down with due to the candy cane-stripped soda straw that poked through the sign's rear edge. And atop the roof stood a giant fiberglass soft-serve cone that beckoned those whose tastes preferred a cold, sweet treat.

Gary and Jack saw that Hilltop was busy with groups of teens hanging around out front on the two picnic tables and that the parking lot was almost full. Gary drove to the far end and steered the Goat into the very last end space, allowing plenty of door room to prevent dings. He didn't notice any sign of the Cyclone as he and Jack got out and walked down to the entrance. Hilltop had huge glass window-walls, and Gary waved to some friends inside as he and Jack dodged a few kids walking by eating ice cream cones. Gary's stomach churned with hunger as he wondered if he should eat or not with the big race upon him. As he opened the door, a waft of French fries frying settled that debate… he'd eat.

Jack made his way to the jukebox as Gary found a seat at a table along the knotty pine-paneled back wall. Two of the three remaining chairs were soon filled by two cute classmates. Jack asked them if they had any requests.

"How about Roy Orbison, Jack?" said Kathy, the cheerful brunette. "I love the song 'Blue Bayou' that he co-wrote with Joe Melson."

"Great song, great voice" agreed Doris. "I'd like to see a female singer pick it up someday."

38

"Let's see here. Blue Bayou. C 34," he replied as he inserted a quarter and pressed the red plastic buttons.

"Hey, that's my bra size, 34 C!" quipped Doris as she threw back her shoulders.

"Too much information!" admonished Kathy as she gave Doris's shoulder a gentle shove.

"No, no," said Gary. "I need all the information I can get! Please, opine away."

"O-pine your mouth Gary and get the waitress over here. We're famished," said Kathy.

Both Kathy and Doris were juniors at the high school and were familiar customers at Hilltop. They were on the cheerleading squad that performed at various sports events and played soft ball in the spring. The high school was modest in size with a little over a hundred students in each grade, so friendships overlapped any grade segregation. In fact, many seniors, especially the guys, dated juniors and even sophomores though the latter was pushing the envelope of current moral norms. After all, what parent would want their sweet sixteen-year-old daughter dating a testosterone-fueled senior?

Doris and Gary hadn't dated but were occasionally part of a boisterous group that attended dances, parties and other extracurricular activities. One notorious activity included driving around the township stealing road signs which required not only some hand tools but an eagle-eyed lookout. This timid gang wasn't known to be a bunch of juvenile delinquents and were, for the most part, honor students. But common sense sometimes eluded their collective minds. Plucking reflective driveway markers while hanging out of the car window was Doris's idea and was a favorite escapade. No tools required, just reach out and pray that the target wasn't stuck in too deep.

One anal homeowner had the audacity to cement the damn things in and once as the car slowed to a crawl, Doris grabbed the red reflector which didn't budge, pulling her almost out the window. If it weren't for Gary's quick jam on the brakes and a firm grab on the belt of her jeans, she'd have been pulled out the window and sprawled across the guy's driveway. That rescue became a highlight of tonight's conversation and was a subtle step closer to a future, more intimate relationship.

"My dad found one of the road signs and two reflectors in our garage," Doris lamented as she sucked on a Coke. "He wasn't too happy. If I hadn't just gotten on the first honors list, I'd have been grounded for a month."

"You said you were going to hide the plunder in your room," said Jack. "And use it to adorn your room at college… if you ever get there."

"Well, plan A didn't work out. I did a female thingy and teared up. Dad just shook his head and walked away. That was plan B."

"Quick thinking there Doris," said Gary. "You're smarter than you…"

"Than you what, Gary?" asked Doris with eyes drilling into Gary's face.

"…than you were last year!"

"Hmmm, nice try. For that you get to buy me a California cheeseburger. No onions."

"That may have to wait," interrupted Jack. "Here comes Dale. I saw the red Cyclone pull up a minute ago. Looks like we're on, Gary."

"On for what?" asked Kathy.

"We're headed out on the bypass to see which car is faster. It'll be a drag race from the Pleasantview Road overpass to that big green "Pottstown Exit" road sign

40

which is about a quarter mile down the way. That is, if no one stole it!"

At that, the group exploded in laughter and agreed that that sign would be the next target... if they could get a big pickup truck and a tall ladder. Dale sauntered up with his friend Tom and took seats at the next table. Dale seemed a bit nervous and didn't want to order any food.

"I saw your Goat parked at the end of the line. I suppose you're ready to get beaten," egged Dale as he drummed his fingers on the table.

"Ha. We'll see about that. Let's lay out the ground rules. We stop side by side under the overpass, windows down, and Jack will count down three, two, one, go. If you jump the gun, you lose. Sound fair?" asked Gary.

"Yeah, that'll work. And the big green sign is the finish line, right?" added Dale.

"Correct. Then meet back here to settle up. By the way, I want a vanilla shake instead of a Coke," demanded Gary.

"You'll have to buy your own as you watch me munch down that burger. And since you're upping the ante, I'll have a chocolate shake."

"Whatever. Let's hit it."

"Gary, can Kathy and I ride with you?" asked Doris.

Gary considered that request for a moment. Having the two girls sitting in the back seat over the rear axle would help cut down on the wheel spin. That extra two hundred pounds or so might give Gary an edge with a good hole shot. But telling them that might insult their feminine concern with weight even though these two were more on the petite side. But if a tire were to blow at ninety miles an hour, he'd never live down what could happen.

41

"Sorry, Doris. No can do. Two guys in each car, that's it."

"Aww. You're a party pooper. I guess we'll just stick around until you get back," lamented Doris.

The guys got up from their chairs and pushed through the crowded tables. Outside the night was clear and warm, and they made their way to their cars. Dale led them out onto the road and immediately lit up his rear tires and blasted away in a cloud of acrid gray smoke that billowed from the rear wheel wells. Gary followed through the haze but refrained from getting on it.

"Geepers. That Cyclone can haul ass. You're gonna have your hands full, Gary," said Jack.

"I'll put that show-off in his place. We both know the cars are pretty even engine wise. It'll come down to the better driver. He will have to shift though, while I'm just hanging on to the steering wheel, feathering the gas pedal at the start and letting the automatic do the rest of the work. I think it'll come down to who gets out of the hole quicker. Maybe I shoudda taken the girls along for the extra weight."

"Too late now," answered Jack.

Gary caught up to Dale's Cyclone as he waited at the entrance to the bypass. Gary flashed his high beams and Dale pulled out and they both headed toward the overpass which was about a mile down the road. The speed limit here was fifty-five miles per hour but Dale kept it at fifty. They needed any cars that came up behind them to pass since they'd be stopping in the middle of a big highway. Three cars overtook them and flashed by. Gary could see about a half mile back in his rearview mirror and seeing no more headlights, pulled up aside of the Cyclone as they came to the overpass starting line and stopped.

"All set?" Jack shouted to Dale.

"Ready." Dale answered as he gunned the engine a few times.

"Gary?"

"Ready."

Jack started the countdown.

"Three…"

"Two.."

Gary's left foot was hard on the brake and his right foot on the gas pedal which he now pushed about halfway down. The car didn't move forward but the body rose a bit and tilted to the right as the torque converter in the transmission dissipated the excess energy. Not a healthy procedure for the Goat but it gave Gary instant power from the start.

"One…"

Dale revved his engine and held it at a high rpm.

"Go!" shouted Jack.

Simultaneously, Gary released the brake, and Dale popped his clutch. They both crammed their right feet into the floor and were off in a thick cloud of smoke as the tires scratched the tarmac for traction. So much for Gary's plan to go easy off the line. The noise from the screaming engines and screeching tires filled their ears as the cars lunged forward. Gary got a three-foot lead as the tires bit. He glanced over as Dale flat-shifted into second gear as his tachometer hit the red line. The Goat was quickly gaining speed and would shift automatically somewhere near its red line at about 5200 rpm which equated to about sixty miles per hour. Gary knew that if he could maintain a lead until then, both cars would be in their highest gear and their final drive line ratios almost even. Then it would be a matter of just hanging on and letting the cars finish the battle.

"We're a half car length ahead, Gary," Jack shouted as he pounded both fists on the padded dash. "Go, go, go!"

"Hey, pick up your feet. You're slowing us down."

Jack laughed and brought his knees to his chest. He stuck his arm out the window and spanked the door like a jockey would whip a racehorse.

"You're going to win, Gary! Just keep it floored."

As the cars approached ninety miles an hour, they were upon the green sign with Gary in the lead by not much more than a short yard. As it flashed past, Gary let off the gas and blew the horn in victory. Dale kept his foot in it and torn down the highway, obviously pissed at losing.

"Oh, Baby! We did it, Jack. We did it!" stammered Gary as the adrenaline coursed through his veins. "I'm about ready to jump out of my skin!"

"You sure did, man. Woo Hoo!"

Gary tested the brakes, they held, and edged over into the right lane to take the quickly approaching exit. Dale on the other hand, deliberately flew by the exit and his red taillights fading into the distance were the last they saw of the Cyclone.

"Think he'll pay up?" Jack asked.

"No matter. I heard that he's not a good sport. Hell, I'll buy everyone a milkshake myself. I've got bragging rights for the next year!"

"That you do. And I'm happy to be in the winning car. GTO's reign!"

They headed back to Hilltop where the crowd had thinned out a bit. Gary pulled the Goat up to the front taking up two spaces. Heads in the crowd turned and started applauding. They instinctively knew who'd won and Gary flashed them a confirming thumbs up. Kathy and Doris walked out, each carrying a milkshake.

"Here ya go Gary," said Doris. "A vanilla trophy for the winner. Congratulations!"

"Jack, here's one for you too," said Kathy. "Was it a close race?"

"It was until I picked my feet up," answered Jack.

"Feet?" the girls said in unison.

"You had to be there," said Jack.

Doris came up close to Gary and gave him a quick kiss and smiled admiringly.

"That's a little something extra for the victor," she said coyly.

"What about me?" quizzed Jack.

"Here ya go," said Kathy as she gave him a peck on the check.

"Well, all right. Let's go race some more! I like this attention," said Jack.

"Nope. That's it for one night. Besides I need some food. Let's go back in and order," said Gary. "I love the smell of French fries in the evening!"

The four of them found seats next to the juke box and placed their orders. In a few minutes, a giant pile of fries commanded the center of the table courtesy of the waitress who'd heard about Gary's victory.

"The fries are on me," she said. "But you'll have to pay up for the burgers."

"No problemo," said Gary. "Just bring us some ketchup, please. And thanks for the free fries. Oh, and how about a little cup of vinegar?"

45

The waitress brought the ketchup and vinegar, and Jack grabbed the squeeze bottle to christen the fries with the ubiquitous ruddy condiment.

"Hey, Jack. Just do half. I like vinegar on mine with lots of salt," said Gary.

"Vinegar on fries? Are you nuts?" Jack replied.

"Yes, vinegar. It's in my Pennsylvania Dutch genes," retorted Gary as he splashed and salted the other half of fries.

"Mmmm. I like 'em that way too," added Doris as she popped one in her mouth. "Ketchup is in a far second place if you ask me. And I'm not even Dutch!"

"I'll take mine with ketchup if it's all the same to you heathens," said Jack. "That is if I can get it out of this squeeze bottle. It must be plugged up."

Jack got a little squirt out of the bottle which he could feel was almost full. He banged it on the table and tried again. But still only a drip came out.

"Whack it harder, Jack. You got big muscles, use 'em," said Gary.

Jack took the hint and lifted the plastic bottle over his head and brought it down on the table with a big whack which got the attention of all the other patrons. His primal effort worked so well that the screw top shot off and hit the ceiling tiles followed by blobs of the contents. Some of the flying ketchup stuck to the ceiling and the rest splattered on Gary, Doris and Kathy. A brief pall of silence came over the room until the comedic scene took hold and everyone broke up laughing. Everyone except the waitress.

"Jack. When we close up later, you'll stick around won't you?" demanded the waitress glumly with her hands on her generous hips. "Actually, that's not just a request."

"That wasn't how I expected to spend the evening

but considering current unforeseen events the answer is yes. And Gary will help me."

"Me? Why me? You're the one who can't control his muscles," said Gary while wiping a blob of ketchup from his cheek.

"Well, guys, nice visiting with you. Have fun at being janitors," said Kathy.

"I'd help but I don't do ketchup as I previously mentioned," added Doris

"I'll tell you what," interrupted Gary. "Help us clean up this mess and we'll take you to the movies tomorrow night. There's a horror flick playing at the Hiway drive-in theater. I think it's Son of Godzilla."

"Oh, Gary, that movie sounds soooo romantic," said Doris. "My heart is fluttering."

"Let's do it, Dor," Kathy suggested. "A bunch of us have been wanting to see it."

"How many in this bunch that you speak of?" asked Gary.

"Let's see," said Kathy counting off her friends mentally. "With us here, I think seven in total."

"The Goat can hold four. Two in the buckets up front and two in the back seat," said Gary.

"Only two in the back?" asked Kathy.

"Yeah, only two seat belts. You could probably wedge in another person in a pinch, but it would be tight.

"We'll need to get a window van. Anyone know who's got one?" asked Jack.

Shaking heads and hunched shoulders were the only responses.

"Let me think," whispered Gary as his eyes searched the red-mottled ceiling for the answer.

"Oh, boy. Here we go. Gary's thinking. Give him room," said Jack as he sat back in his chair.

"Got it!" Gary proudly stated. "We'll meet here Saturday before the movie."

"That's your big idea?"

"It gets better, but I'll leave the good part 'til then.

CHAPTER FIVE

With both of them primed from the car show, the hunt began in earnest. Jo showed Gary the ins and outs of online searching and bidding, and she even set up an account for Gary that allowed him to bid directly. Each week they would check the classic car inventory to see if a restorable GTO would show up. A few did but were quickly prebid beyond Gary's limit of $2800... which was all he could scrape together without Doris finding out and throwing a hissy fit. A few weeks went by without any prospects. Laboring over the computer one morning, Gary is getting bummed out and Jo is doing her best to be compassionate. She even cooked him a special breakfast since Doris had gone to the farmer's market early. The two eggs Benedict stared up at him from the plate.

"This breakfast looks real good, Jo. It's my favorite as you well know."

"Happy to be of service. I was gonna do the eggs royale bit but couldn't find good lox."

"Yeah, you remembered the story where we went on that almost free cruise, and I ate eggs royale every day. Ain't doin' that again anytime soon. Can't afford it now."

"I've never been on a cruise. Did you like it?"

"It helped being a cheap vacation. Some friends had

booked the cruise but couldn't go due to illness, so they offered it to us for half price."

"An offer you couldn't refuse," said Jo in her mafioso voice.

"Precisely. I was hesitant to go at first. You know I don't do crowds, but I decided to get my head in the right place, and it worked out well."

"It's all about perception. You chose to have a good time, and you did."

"I do try to live by the saying 'the only handicap in life is a bad attitude'. Maybe it's the stoic in me. Perception is a choice."

Gary took a bite and relished the Hollandaise sauce which really set this meal apart. Nodding his head yes, he smiled at Jo but something was troubling him.

"I don't know Jo. I'm thinking I might never find a GTO that I can afford. They are pretty rare as it is let alone finding a rust bucket that I can restore," said Gary as he tried in vain to twist off a beer bottle cap.

"Starting a bit early today aren't you, Gary? You comin' over to the dark side?" asked Jo between sips of her own Yuengling.

"It's Saturday. It's 9:30. And we're out of orange juice. What's a guy supposed to do?"

"I should make you a Bloody Mary. They're great with eggs."

"We're out of tomato juice, too. And out of luck on the car hunt."

"We're not giving up. Eventually the right car will show up. Like wine, good things take time," comforted Jo as she grabbed his bottle, dug a church key out of her pocket and flipped off the cap.

"Time yes, but mostly money. The whole world can

50

bid on these cars and there are deep pockets out there. Jay Leno can afford to buy any car he wants, but me... that's another story."

"Keep the faith my friend. Be patient. Your Goat will come in due time. Hee Haw, Hee Haw," Jo mimicked.

"I think that would be a donkey. Goats go baaahh... no wait, sheep go baaahh. What do goats do?"

"Hell if I know. Do I look like a farmer?" asked Jo.

"No comment. Well, my Goat's gonna go 'varooomm! On with the hunt!"

They clinked their beer bottles together, Gary finished his breakfast, and they got back on the computer.

CHAPTER SIX

On Saturday night after the big race, Gary asked for the car to take the clan to the Hiway drive-in movie located just down the road from Hilltop. 'Just be home by 12:00 and put some gas in it' were dad's only and usual requests. Hmmm, Gary thought… gas money, tickets, popcorn and a Coke… this could be beyond his meager means, but he couldn't renege on his promise.

Gary and his friends met at Hilltop about an hour before the start of the movie. He'd picked up the guys, and Karen had volunteered to bring Doris and Kathy. Parked next to each other, they then huddled around Gary as he explained his grand idea.

"So, the GTO can hold four people, usually," Gary said with a wry smile.

"Usually?" questioned Doris.

"Yeah, two in front, two in back. Allotting for all the seat belts."

"So, expound more on the 'usually'," Doris demanded.

The trunk of the GTO was quite spacious especially if you removed the spare tire which crowded the right side. Gary sized up the girls, opened the trunk and did some rough calculations in his head. Fortunately, the three girls, Doris, Kathy and Karen, were quite petite and with the proper contortions, could probably fit into the trunk. Gary was really liking this scheme.

"Jesus mini, Gary. I'm not about to climb into that trunk," proclaimed Doris having read his mind.

"Me neither," said Karen. "What kind of nuts are you?

"Why don't the guys get in the trunk? They seem to be as clueless as you Gary," said Kathy as she stared down the guys who looked innocently at each other.

"Wait a second. Hold on there ladies. First of all, the guys are too big. Heck, Tom and Bob are each over 200 pounds. And Jim's about 180, so with all that weight way back in the rear, the Goat would be doin' wheelies down the road. That's twice the weight that it can handle. Since you gals are so petite, it is fitting that you should be the ones to get in the trunk."

"So let me get this straight, Gary," puzzled Doris. "We three girls jam ourselves into that trunk, shut the lid, and you drive us down to the movies just to save the admission fee. Is that it?"

"Basically, yeah. Great idea, huh?"

"I wouldn't get in there if you paid me," said Kathy.

"I might for a chocolate shake," conceded Karen.

"One down, two to go," said Jack.

"You stay out of this, Jack. I'll bet you think it's a great idea too," said Doris. "Karen, would you really agree to doing this?"

"I like chocolate shakes, especially if they're free. Heck, it's only about two miles to the drive-in. We'd be in and out in five minutes. Where's your sense of larceny?"

"Well, maybe," said Kathy. "Can I get fries with that?"

"Jesus mini! You two are crazy," proclaimed Doris as she stood there hands on hips.

"Who's this Jesus mini?" asked Gary.

"My mom has a little Jesus figurine on her dashboard which I called Jesus mini when I was seven. I now say it when I'm flustered. Which I am right now."

"Oh, come on Doris," said Karen. "It'll be fun and exciting."

"Yeah, Doris. Let's do it!" added Kathy.

Doris thought for a moment and looked around at the six pairs of eyes awaiting her decision. Gary glanced at his wristwatch and tapped its face. Time was a waisting.

"Oh, all right. You two are as nuts as the guys. How do we do this?" Doris relented.

"Fantastic!" said Gary. "Jack, get the spare tire out and put in the trunk of Karen's car. Bob, you take the girls in for the shakes. I'll pay you back next week."

With the trunk completely empty and the girls' stomachs growing full, they went about discussing how this was going to work.

"Let's see," said Gary. "You're all about the same size, so how about if Doris gets in first?"

"Why me? Karen was the one who caved in for a chocolate shake."

"Ok, then. Karen, be my guest," said Gary as he offered his hand to help her in.

Karen put a leg over the rear valance and awkwardly rolled into the trunk. She lay there on her back looking up at Gary.

"Perfectly done, Karen," smiled Gary. "Scrunch over to one side and put your head up on the rear shelf. Good. Good. You're next Kathy. Spoon in next to Karen."

Kathy legged over the valance but got stuck halfway in when the button on her jeans caught the trunk latch. She lurched backward and the button went flying.

"So much for my new jeans," frowned Kathy. "Maybe this isn't such a great idea."

"You'll be fine," said Karen as she patted the trunk floor beside her. "Come snuggle."

And she did. Karen put her arm around Kathy and they both giggled and motioned for Doris to get in. The trunk, however, now seemed smaller as the two stowaways took up most of the room. Doris would be a tight fit.

"Scrunch over more you two," demanded Doris. "I'm not sure I'll fit in there."

"Come on, come on. We gotta get a move on. Godzilla waits for no one. Get in there Doris," urged Gary.

"I knew I shudda worn jeans. You guys stand over there and don't look up my skirt as I get in."

The guys all moved away in dejected mumbles as Doris lifted a leg over, shifted her weight into the trunk and crashed heavily onto the two captives whose feigned owws and ohhs gave way to spontaneous giggles. Doris tugged fruitlessly at her skirt sensing Gary's widening eyes, but managed to squeeze in beside Kathy. They nudged, pinched and teased each other as they tried to get as comfortable as the trio could in the trunk of a car.

"Three peas in a pod," proclaimed Gary. "Giggly peas. You'll have to be very quiet when we get to the movies. No noise whatsoever!"

"Yeah, we get it. Now let's get this over with. I'm already cramping up," said Karen.

"Get off my arm, Doris. And Karen, enough with the tickling or I'm going to throw up my milkshake."

"Ok, that's it. Pipe down now. I'm going to close the lid and get going," said Gary.

He gently shut the lid and inside of the trunk became pitch black which elicited muffled groans from the girls.

"You ok in there?" asked Gary as he knocked gently on the trunk lid.

"I didn't think about it being dark," said a faint voice. "This is very weird."

"You'll be fine. I'm going to start the car. I'll let you know when we get to the ticket box."

Gary and the guys piled into the Goat. He could tell right away that the rear end was riding a bit lower and hoped that the ticket man wouldn't notice. After all, it wasn't the first time that anyone had snuck into a drive-in movie. As he pulled onto Rt 422 heading east, he had to give it a little more gas than usual and when he hit a bump the shocks bottomed out with a metallic clunk. He glanced over a Jack who shrugged his shoulders and motioned to keep going.

This area of the road was notorious for potholes causing Gary to pay particular attention. As twilight dimmed the skies, Gary flicked on the headlights which because of the higher front rake, the low beams shone as high. An oncoming car flicked his lights signaling the courtesy to dim your bright lights, but Gary could do nothing. Just wince and squint as the car went by. The next oncoming car did the same but seeing no response, kept his highs on as punishment. He even blew his horn as he passed.

"Gary, you're pissing off everyone," said Jack.

"What am I supposed to do? I need lights."

The third oncoming car also flashed Gary. But this time Gary flashed back to signal that he already had his lows on. The Goat's high beams lit up the sky and blinded the other driver who coasted into Gary's lane. Gary edged over to the right just in time to make acquaintance with what was apparently the largest pothole in Pennsylvania. Boom, Boom. Both right side tires sounded a direct hit, and the car bounced high enough to squeeze the seat belts on the guys. The peas were momentarily airborne and jostled in the hard confines of the trunk.

"That wasn't good," Jack admitted.

"No. And the peas aren't happy. Bob, yell back to see if they're ok."

"You ok back there?" Bob questioned as he turned his head and shouted at the rear shelf behind the seat.

"Yeah, we're ok. That was kinda loud back here and something doesn't sound right," came the muted response.

"Something doesn't feel right either," worried Gary. "I'm going to pull over to check things out."

Gary eased the Goat into the parking lot of a closed furniture store and the guys all got out to survey for any damage. The right front seemed ok if you overlooked the mud splash. The right rear was another story however. The rim displayed a small dent, and the wheel cover was ajar. The tire was worse for the wear displaying some delaminated rubber that signaled its coming demise.

"Tire's shot," said Jack. "But it's still holding air. For now."

"And the spare is back at Hilltop," said Gary. "Son of a sea cook. Dad'll be pissed."

Gary keyed the trunk lock and opened the lid.

"You all ok in there?" he asked.

"Yeah, we're good," they answered in surprised unison which made them start to giggle.

"How far to the movie?" Karen asked.

"But can we get there?" Doris questioned.

"It's just a mile more," Gary said. "I think we should

still try to make it. The tire is holding air and everything else is good."

"Jesus mini, Gary. Clam us back up and get movin'," demanded Doris. "Before I get out and start walkin'."

"Yes, mam! I don't want your little Jesus to get on my case," smiled Gary as he shut the trunk lid. "Jack, bang that rim back on tight and the rest of you guys jump back in. Godzilla here we come!"

Gary limped the Goat to the drive-in's entrance and pulled up behind a line of three cars waiting to get in. Gary switched to his parking lights to avoid drenching the car in front in light and hopefully avoid undue attention of the ticket man. It wasn't unusual to see a hot car jacked up in the front because hot rodders wanted to shift weight to the rear wheels for better traction. But this Goat didn't really look hot roddish having no mag wheels, over-wide tires nor 'STP' decals on the windows. Except for the weight-induced rake, it was fairly demure albeit powerful.

"Bob, tell the girls we're here and to keep quiet," Gary requested.

Turning over his shoulder, Bob rapped twice on the back deck and said "We're here so put a sock in it." The response was a few muffled giggles and then shhh, shhh.

Gary pulled up to the ticket booth and rolled down the window.

"How many?" asked the young attendant.

"Four," Gary lied.

"That will be two dollars, please."

Gary handed him eight quarters and got four tickets in return.

"The feature movie hasn't started yet, just the coming attractions so you're just in time. Would you like to fill out a card for a free ticket? The drawing is at the end of the movie."

"Heck yeah," said Gary. "Let me have it."

Gary was handed the card and a plastic ballpoint pen, filled in this name and phone number and handed it back but fumbled with the pen and it dropped down under the side of his seat.

"That's ok," the attendant remarked. "I'll just take the card, you can keep the pen. We're giving them away tonight anyway. Nice car by the way."

"Thanks," Gary said as he put it in drive and pulled away.

Gary drove through the field of cars to one of the speaker poles in the back row, empty except for a Chevy with fogged windows three places over. The guys got out and Gary keyed the trunk and lifted the lid.

"You girls did great. Let's get you out and watch the movie," said Gary.

They spread an Army blanket on the ground next to the Goat while two of the guys walked up to the refreshment stand to get popcorn and sodas. They chatted and told jokes as Godzilla and his son defeated the abominable giant insects. After the movie ended, the girls refused to get back in the trunk and instead sat on the laps of the three guys. They all waved at the attendant on the way out as Gary quickly drove by.

"Hey. You won the contest!" he shouted at them waving a ticket. Seeing the car stuffed full he said to himself. "Well, I guess we're all even then."

Gary and Doris had many mutual friends and adventures, but a romantic spark between them had not

59

yet sprung to life. That of course would come later. But when he helped her into the trunk of the GTO that night, their eyes met for more than a moment, and something clicked between them. Their casual date prompted Gary to eventually track down her phone number and, if courage permitted, make the call.

CHAPTER SEVEN

All the while Gary and Jo were conniving to buy a GTO, Doris went about her normal routine of working as a nurse, doing her share of the chores around the house, taking Nicky for a walk and wishing to hit the lottery for a hundred grand. She wasn't greedy for the mega gazillions, but just enough to pay off the debts and put them a step closer to easy street.

Having moved into their rancher many years ago, there were still boxes that hadn't been opened. Many of the boxes were labeled as to contents and could be found in the dark corner of a bedroom closet or stacked neatly in the low attic. Most, however, were in the big closet in the basement that Gary had framed out right after the house was purchased. Wooden shelves lined both sides with a narrow aisle down the middle which was hardly navigable because it became a repository for the bigger things that wouldn't fit on the shelves... bushy floral wreaths, the huge spider web Halloween decoration, an old vacuum cleaner, a heavy guitar amp and various large vases. With a single door and no windows, air circulation still wasn't the best even after Gary cut two vents in the wall. He'd get around to installing an electric fan for more air exchange someday.

Though far from being a neatness freak, Doris decided to clean out this big basement closet as a goal to accomplish before the weekend. On the previous day, she was trying to find a box of old photos that had been hidden away in this tomb and after removing box after box of Christmas ornaments, two old sleeping bags, various and sundry bare picture frames, and Gary's old guitar amp, she thought enough is enough. Time to girl up and throw away the crap that hasn't been used in years and neatly, for once, rearrange the good stuff with enough room to maneuver without twisting an ankle.

Some of these cardboard boxes hadn't been opened in ten years and were getting a funky musty smell which didn't help her allergies one bit. After a sneeze or two and a wipe of her runny nose on her flannel shirt sleeve, she started carrying the boxes out into the rec room. With the many boxes and ephemera to decide upon, she decided on a simple triage… keep and not keep. Of course, her boxes were favored as keepers, Gary's not so much. Her high school yearbooks and varsity letters… keepers. Gary's old black and whites from a college photography course… not keep. Nicky was pacing nearby and helping by staying out of her way. He sniffed at the stale sleeping bags as a potential place to curl up, but his sensitive nose would have nothing of it. Instead, he plopped down on her hoodie that she'd removed and thrown on the floor. After two hours of decisions and distractions, she got to the point where fatigue trumped rational thinking and most of the remainder enlarged the 'not keep' pile. Her neighbor Maggie called to say she was coming over to chat and was there in two minutes.

"Looks like you've finally lost your mind" Maggie remarked as she scanned the basement floor.

"I have. It's gotta be in one of these two piles… help me look."

"Needle in a haystack I'd say. So, what gives?"

"I just couldn't stand the clutter in the big closet so here I am. Two piles... keep and not keep."

"Lemme guess. The big pile is the not keep and is mostly Gary's stuff."

Doris' playful smirk triggered the reply.

"He won't miss it. Hell, he can't remember what he had for dinner last night."

"But he is somewhat nostalgic, no? He likes old stuff... cars, history, leftovers."

"He has no trouble in reminding me to get rid of my old clothes that take up half our bedroom closet. He won't care."

"Have you even opened some of the Gary-labeled boxes?"

"One or two, but that got old quick. Unless it has 'do not destroy' written in bold magic marker, it's outta here."

"Your call but I do believe that Gary does have a sentimental streak."

"Oh well, then he should be down here helping sort things out. I did ask him, but he left it to my discretion, him having to run off to get in nine holes with Burt."

"Any witnesses to that remark?"

"Just Nicky. I gave him a dog treat to seal his allegiance."

Nicky's ear perked up as he licked his chops.

"Good thinkin'. He won't say a thing."

"Nicky loves everyone, but his lips are sealed... unless a treat is involved," Doris said as she reached in her pocket and tossed a kibble to him.

"Keep 'em handy if push comes to shove about throwing out Gary's stuff."

"Now that you're here, Maggie, lend a hand and carry the no keepers out to my car. We'll load up the back and take it to Goodwill. Then we can grab brunch and a margarita at Sammy's… my treat."

"To quote Gary… oh baby!"

As Maggie was loading the van, her curiosity prodded her to open some of the boxes just to see what was being discarded. A box of old textbooks provided no interest nor did a box of old toy cars and parts. The one with pants and shirts folded atop each other held her attention briefly, as did the funky blue shoes at the very bottom, but then Doris came out with her arms full, so Maggie closed the lid and went to give Doris a hand.

"See anything you want?" Doris asked.

"Nope. Just nosing around. I saw some nice blue shoes, but they were men's. Are you sure you want this stuff Goodwilled? It might be useful someday."

"Doubtful that day will ever come. No, out it goes."

Having finished loading the car, they jumped in and headed straight for the Goodwill store over on Lancaster Avenue about a mile away. There they unloaded and got a donation receipt, then headed over to Sammy's as promised.

"Well, that was easy," Doris said while pulling out of the Goodwill lot. "I shoulda done that five years ago. I feel like a big load has been lifted from my shoulders."

"That was a big pile of stuff. I hope Gary doesn't mind that you threw out some of his things."

"Like I said. He had his chance, and I have Nicky as my witness."

"I hope they don't have to swear in Nicky at the divorce proceedings."

"Enough already. I can handle Gary as you well know. When we're done at Sammy's can you help me repack the closet?

"Sure. But then I have a new recipe to show you… Bumbleberry pie!"

Sammy's restaurant was nestled between an artist studio and an ice cream parlor along the busy Penn Avenue. Various and sundry shops, bars and restaurants lined both sides of the street in this recently gentrified borough just over the river from the city proper. Parking took two trips around the block before a spot opened right in front of Sammy's.

"Hah! What timing," Doris declared putting on her right turn signal to indicate her intentions.

"We coulda just parked in the lot down the street and saved time and gas doing those loop-de-loos around the block" Maggie said.

"But then we'd have to deal with walking after having a margarita. Or two."

"Promise to give our waitress your car keys with explicit instructions to return them when sober."

"Janey knows us well enough. She won't take her tip until we can walk straight and count backwards from ten."

"That counting has been a challenge in the past as I recall. Last time it was a two hour wait."

"That was your birthday and cause for celebration. We stayed here the entire afternoon playing shuffleboard, eating duck fat fries, and checking out the young studs that came by for lunch."

"What happens at Sammy's, stays at Sammy's" Maggie interjected.

"We really embarrassed those guys. A bunch of

raucous, middle-aged dames flirting with good-looking twenty-somethings. A day that will live in infamy."

Brunch at Sammy's was a popular affair especially on Fridays. The bar was open and those folks who wanted to get a start on a partying weekend looked no further than Sammy's. The spicy Bloody Mary's went well with eggs, and the flight of margaritas, Doris and Maggie's favorite, fit perfectly with the fish tacos. If you hadn't eaten breakfast, either of those drinks would set the stage for the rest of the afternoon. 'It's five o'clock somewhere' was the refrain heard regularly before ten a.m. at Sammy's.

As they pushed in the front door, Janey caught their eye and motioned to a table for two near the window, their favorite seat. The smells of bacon frying, and sourdough bread baking made their mouths water and their empty stomachs grumble. Maggie gave a thumbs up and a wink to Janey who knew the code and nodded with a smile. Within a minute the potent margaritas were delivered and sipped.

"Ohhh… these are sooo good" Doris whispered.

"What's the occasion?" asked Janey, order pad in hand.

"We cleaned out a closet" Maggie answered.

"Oh. The bar for celebration has slipped down a rung," Janey remarked.

"You know us. Always looking for new levels of debauchery," Doris said.

"I'll put in an order of fish tacos, stat! And take little sips until they get here."

They nodded in agreement, giggled, and put the salted rims to their waiting lips.

CHAPTER EIGHT

Though seventeen-year-old Gary was a gregarious, popular guy, he was quite shy when it came to women and the notion of 'going steady' didn't register on his agenda. Just asking a girl for a date would be a terrifying ordeal. Take going to a prom for example. First, he'd have to find out if a candidate was uncommitted by deftly probing one of her friends without being too obvious about his intentions. Having received an 'all clear', he wouldn't address her directly but call her on the phone instead. The phone... the black demon with a rotary dial that provided not only a direct link but also a heavy dose of intimidation.

The only phone in his parent's home was in a small hallway between the bedrooms, bathroom and kitchen. It rested on a colonial-style telephone table with a conjoining seat. And he'd have to wait until his parents were out of the house to have any modicum of privacy. Who in their right mind would want their parents to eavesdrop on an intimate conversation? Gary would sit and stare at the phone as his nerves started to fray. What if she said no? How would he handle the rejection? How many times had he started to dial but bailed out halfway through?

Get a grip on yourself he thought. Am I a wuss or what? So, after summoning up every ounce of courage he could muster, he dialed the entire number and listened intently as the ringing sound pulsed in his ear. One ring… silence. The second ring… silence. The third ring…

"Hello?" answered Doris's mom.

"Ah, uh, hi. This is Gary Miller. Would Doris be home?"

"Why yes, Gary. She's home. Let me get her."

Gary could barely hear her summoning Doris over the sound of his heart pounding in his chest.

"Doris, it's Gary Miller on the phone for you. Can you take the call?"

"Ok, mom. I'll be right there," Doris answered distantly.

So far, so good thought Gary. At least she didn't pretend she wasn't home. Gary had prepared a script in his head which was now as effective as a balled-up sheet of paper in a wastebasket. He'd have to wing it.

"Hello. This is Doris," she said.

"Hi, Doris. It's Gary. How ya doin'?"

"Ahh, I'm fine Gary. How are *you* doing."

"I'm well. Thanks for askin'," stammered Gary.

"Soooo, what's up?"

"Ah, I, ah, wondered if you'd like to go to the Big Mug coffee shop on Sunday afternoon. They have this trio playing at two o'clock. I think you mentioned that you like bluegrass music."

"I love bluegrass. But I don't know if I can make it. I have church in the morning and choir practice until about 1:30 or so. Where is the Big Mug located?"

"It's about a half hour of so north up Route 61 a ways. They'll be playing until about five o'clock so we can get there anytime."

"Hmm. Let me ask mom if there is anything she needs me to do. Hold on a sec."

Gary's blood pressure had moderated to sub-critical, and his heart slowed perceptively below sprint race level albeit with an occasional skip thrown in for good measure. He absentmindedly wiped a bead of sweat from his forehead. The peak of the crisis had passed and now if she'd only agree to the date, he'd be able to crash on the sofa and watch the Sixer's game without really caring who won.

"Gary? Mom said that I'm free Sunday afternoon. She and dad are going to visit my aunt in Womelsdorf. I just have to take Teeny out for a short walk to do his business."

"Teeny is your mutt that weighs about eighty pounds, right?" Gary asked.

"That's him. The world's best mutt if I do say so myself. You can hold the leash."

"So, you're going. That's fantastic. Speaking of dogs, if you want, we can catch a hot dog on the way home."

"Ok, whatever works. So, stop by at 2:00 which should give me time to freshen up a bit."

"I wouldn't think that choir practice would be that exhausting."

"The choir director is very demanding. I'm beat mentally after singing the same song until we get it right. Sometimes five or six complete go-throughs. And my feet start to ache after standing for an hour."

"I guess I'm lucky that I can't hold a tune," said Gary.

"I suppose it's worth it in the long run. Especially at Christmas. That's the best time."

"I'll look forward to coming to your concerts. Well, ok then. Two o'clock it is. I'll have the Goat cleaned up and I'll see you then.

"Wait. We're riding an animal to the gig?" she questioned.

"The car's model is GTO. We motorheads pronounce it Goat."

"Ok, Gary. That's more like it. Thanks for calling me. It'll be fun. Bye now."

"Ok, bye."

Gary deftly replaced the phone back on its receiver and closed his eyes and let out a deep breath. He'd done it. And all that anxiety was a distant memory now. It really wasn't that hard after all. The next time would be easier. Assuming there was a next time, and he didn't screw up the date. Time will tell and Sunday would be here soon enough.

Sunday morning dawned to clear blue skies with puffy cumulous clouds drifting slowly eastward in the light breeze. It had drizzled overnight and although he'd washed the GTO on Friday, he wanted it to be perfect for his date with Doris. The garage that his dad was having built would be the future home for the Goat, but until that was finished, the car was subjected to the elements. Water spots on the windshield wouldn't do, nor on the chrome bumpers and wheel covers. With a small bucket of clean water, he dampened a sponge and methodically went over the entire car. A dry towel finished the job. A few squirts of Windex took care of the windows and perhaps a puff of 'new car' scent would freshen up the interior. But then, Gary thought, it was a new car so why be redundant? What scent would Doris like? Fresh mint? Orange citrus? And would they compete with the Canoe cologne that he'd plan to splash on? He ended up peeling off the plastic wrapper of a Christmas tree air freshener, a free token from Waltz's tree farm, and pushed it up under that dash as not to be noticed. The fresh air vents would tease the aroma from the tree and add a subtle fragrance that he hoped Doris would enjoy.

The rest of the interior was spotless, and he'd even hand-picked the lint off the black carpet which ran between the bucket seats, the Goat having no center console. Without thinking, he sprayed lemon-scented polish on the wood dash and rubbed it in. Doh! Rolling down the windows the gentle breeze should air that pungent odor out in a few minutes. Looking around while sitting in the driver's seat, he felt as though he had all the bases covered. All he had to do now was bide his time until he had to pick up Doris.

It was only about two miles to Doris' house, so he left to pick her up at about a quarter to two, deftly avoiding any puddled potholes lest they mess up all his morning's elbow grease and sweat. He dodged a gray squirrel which had the audacity to bolt right out in front of him. The stupid rodent ran halfway across then abruptly stopped and ran back from whence he came, right in the Goat's path. Gary did a quick swerve and missed the little bugger, but the brief shot of adrenalin put all his senses on Red Alert. He hoped he'd calm down a bit by the time he got to Doris' place. He popped a stick of Juicy Fruit into his mouth and drummed his fingers on the steering wheel, a Bo Diddley tune providing the rhythm…'shave and a haircut, two bits'.

Pulling the shiny Pontiac onto her driveway, he put it in park and doused the engine. The split level was part of a nice, suburban community and Gary returned the wave from the next-door neighbor who was watering his lush, green lawn. Climbing the three steps to the front door, he pressed the white button on the door's frame but couldn't hear if the doorbell rang so he waited a few seconds and then gave a tentative tap, tap, tap.

"Oh, hi, Mr. Impatient," said Doris as she opened the door.

"Sorry 'bout that, Doris. I couldn't hear the doorbell. You look wonderful by the way."

Doris's well-worn denim skirt stood in stark contrast with the crisp white cotton blouse that accentuated her ample bosom. A dainty jeweled necklace adorned her thin neck, and her long blonde ponytail draped over one shoulder. Gary appreciated the dichotomy of her clothing and when the faint aroma of lilac drifted by, he decided that heaven had come to earth. He stood there almost comatose.

"Gary. You good?" she asked cocking her head slightly to one side.

"Absolutely," Gary answered as he blinked his eyes into focus. "Never better. Are you ready to boogie?"

"I thought you said it was a bluegrass gig," she quipped.

"Ha, ha. We chillen gonna boogie to bluegrass."

"Mom," Doris called over her shoulder. "Gary's here and we're going to leave now. I've already taken Teeny for his walk."

"Ok, be careful and have fun," replied a distant voice. "Drive gently Gary."

"Sure thing Mrs. Riley. Have a nice day."

"It looks like you got the dress code memo, Gary. We look like twins," she said eyeing his jeans and chalky Henley shirt. "I'll take a purse so folks can tell us apart."

Doris grabbed a small, sequined red leather shoulder bag which completed her all-American appearance. Gary gently took her hand and led her to the passenger's side of the Goat. He opened the door, and Doris nodded approval and daintily got in. In doing so, her skirt rose halfway up her thighs to which she gave a half-hearted tug. Gary gently closed the door and wondered what lay in store for the rest of the day… and evening.'

Gary walked around to the driver's side and gave a hearty wave to Doris's mom who'd come to the front picture window to watch them leave. She pointed at the car and flashed a thumbs up. Gary smiled, nodded and returned the gesture. As he plopped down on the bucket seat, he fastened the seat belt, pulled it snug and started the car. Backing out of the driveway, they headed to the coffee shop with the windows rolled down.

"I L-O-V-E this car," Doris spelled as she looked over the interior and caressed the leather seat that held her tanned thighs. "Isn't that new car smell great? And a little piney too."

"Yeah," agreed Gary but didn't expound. "And that's lovely perfume you're wearing."

"Thanks. It's just a splash of lilac. I'm glad you like it. I detected a nice scent on you. What is it?"

"Canoe, canoe?" quizzed Gary just like on the TV ad.

"Ah, yes. Canoe. I like it. Most guys drench themselves in English Leather which makes me want to gag. Not the scent, the amount," she said fanning her nose in jest.

"I just use a drop or two, not wanting to smell like a French whore."

"Oh? I didn't know you've been to France. Did you lose your virginity there?"

Gary was perplexed by this conversational detour into the sexual realm which made him uncomfortable to say the least. He was just trying to make a joke but perhaps his timing was off. And those thighs were still staring back at him. He hesitated in answering for a beat.

"Gary? This pregnant pause is disconcerting. Speak up."

Pregnant? There she goes with the sex thing again he thought.

"Uh, none of the above. It was just a figure of speech that I heard from my brother's friend a few years ago. I was in the back seat as we drove to a baseball game. I had overdone an application of Brut cologne, and they were making fun of me. At fourteen, you have a lot of learning to do."

"You've evidently come a long way. You're much cooler now," she smiled.

The bluegrass and herbal teas on the Big Mug's outdoor patio made for a perfect Sunday afternoon. It had been a busy, half hour drive up and Gary decided to take a more scenic route home. Along the way, they stopped for hot dogs and soda.

"What do you want on your dog?" Gary asked.

"Nothing."

"Nothing? How about some sauerkraut?"

"No thanks. Just plain please."

"Ok, suit yourself. I like kraut and mustard."

"The Pennsyvania Dutch thing again I suspect. I hold the line at vinegar on fries."

"Yeah, but there's pork and sauerkraut for New Year's Day. You should come try it."

"If that's an invitation, I'll take it."

That's a few months away, Gary thought as they

munched the hot dogs and motored down the deserted roadway. Maybe we'd be going steady by then. Hallelujah, he muttered to himself with another glance at those alluring thighs. She detected his glimpse but refrained from adjusting her skirt and instead unfastened her seat belt.

"I feel like your sister sitting way over here," she mused as she slid over toward Gary, now half on the gap between the seats and almost thigh to thigh.

"Uh, that's not safe," muttered Gary.

"Don't you like me sitting right next to you?"

"Absolutely. I'm just sayin'…"

"You're a good driver, Gary. I think we'll be ok. I'm happier sitting here."

"Theres's a parking lot for a trail access down the road a piece," suggested Gary as he eyed the rear seat. "It's usually pretty quiet."

"Hmmm," she said glancing over her shoulder. "I'm still burping up that hot dog. How about later?"

"Yeah, right, later. That works!" stumbled Gary. "Later works good."

Gary smiled and reached for the radio to change the station keeping one eye on the road. He pressed one of the preset buttons, but she then pressed another. Then he pressed one, and she another. Back and forth this went as they fooled around, and she'd even taken a nibble at his hand at one point. Claiming victory, she selected an AM station that was playing country tunes. They were halfway through singing along with Johnny Cash when a huge whitetail buck darted from the dense forest and right in front of the Goat. Tires screeched and Gary quickly turned the steering wheel to the right as the deer bounded over the hood. The car veered off the road and Gary counter-steered but to no avail. The Goat slid into a shallow ditch and bounced hard over a large rock as Gary grabbed Doris tightly with his strong right arm, realizing that she wasn't strapped in. A huge oak tree stopped them abruptly as everything loose in the car went airborne, including the Coke that Doris had been sipping on. Her butt slid forward just enough to reveal the rest of her thighs, and her jeweled necklace unclasped itself and went flying.

Now stopped and startled, a shaky silence overwhelmed them. Gary released his firm grip on the wheel and on Doris. A wisp of steam rose from under the crumpled hood as Gary unclipped his seat belt.

"You ok?" Gary stammered.

"Yeah, I think so. You saved me from hitting the dashboard."

"We won't say anything about your not wearing a seatbelt. Agreed?"

"Agreed."

"Let's get out of here. I don't see any fire, but let's not wait around to find out."

The Goat was mainly intact except for the front end, but the impact had jostled the entire body. Gary had to shoulder the door open and push it out with his foot. He awkwardly climbed out and turned to help Doris as she crawled over the driver's seat. They walked back from the steaming car and stood arm in arm in dismay.

Gary looked back up the road but didn't see the deer which had disappeared into a tangled thicket of brush. Twin black skids marked the road and continued onto the berm. An oily slick started at the scratched rock and disappeared under the car. He knew that meant big trouble with the underside. A passing motorist slowed down and pulled over to ask if they were alright and then offered them a lift to his house to use the phone.

"Mom, I'm ok but we had a little accident with the car," Doris explained. "Gary's dad is going to pick us up and I should be home in about an hour. Yes, yes, I'm fine and so is Gary. Ok, see you soon, bye."

"Your mom's ok with it?" asked Gary.

"Yeah, she knows I don't fib about serious things. She's just happy that we're not hurt."

"So are my parents," added Gary. "Dad always says that cars are replaceable, people aren't. I'm kinda glad it was a deer and not just me screwing up. Hey look," discovered Gary as he apprised both of their mottled shirts. "We've got matching Coke stains!"

Doris looked down at her blouse and then at Gary's blotched shirt as they laughed their anxiety away. Gary always sees the brighter side she thought. Maybe he's the one.

Gary's dad had called AAA after hearing the bad news and arranged for the disabled car to be picked up. They all met at the accident scene to watch as the Goat was winched up onto a rollback truck. Oil wept from the engine making a growing, dark puddle on the bed of the truck which was destined to the dealer where his dad had purchased it.

As they watched the truck rumble away, Doris had her arms crossed and fidgeted with her blouse collar as she was wont to do when nervous. A finger sensed the missing necklace, but she thought little of it being happy to get out of the wreck unscathed.

After a thorough assessment of the damaged car, the dealership and the insurance company agreed that the car could be repaired but the cost was sky high. Dad really didn't want to drive a car that had so much damage and chose to replace it with another Pontiac sedan albeit without the GTO badging. The forlorn Goat ended up being sold off and the memories it created were relegated to the annals of history. Gary often pondered what adventures the Goat might have brought to him and Doris, but alas, it apparently wasn't in the cards.

CHAPTER NINE

Gary logged on early one morning only to find a rusty but running 1966 Goat. And it was located within a day's drive of his house. 'Ran when parked' was the key feature that got his attention, and it was a complete car, lacking no major parts. A shabby interior, bruised bumpers, and a dented and rust-perforated body completed Gary's check list of items that would dissuade many potential bidders. It was an automatic, but Gary wasn't fussy. Somebody at one time had given it a lousy blue paint job and had generally hogged up what was once a beautiful muscle car. But in Gary's eyes he had found the motherlode. He grabbed his cell phone and misdialed Jo three times in his excitement. When he finally got through, he was unable to contain his enthusiasm.

"Jo? Gary. Guess what I found?"

"*The* car?" replied Jo.

"Yep. *THE* car. Looks like crap but finally after all this hunting, here she is."

"Do tell me more!"

"It's got most of its parts and catch this: 'ran when parked'."

"Yeah? Parked when?"

"About fifteen years ago. Been sitting in a dry barn, and it's covered in dust, pigeon poop and has a mouse nest in the trunk. Oh baby!"

79

"When's the auction?"

"Next Saturday, 10:00 a.m. There are already a few preliminary bids. The bid history shows two guys are after it so far… Goatman and Chief Pontiac.

"Uh oh. Those are two serious bidders to have monikers like that. They gotta have a lot of experience and probably already own one or two or three… who knows?"

"Yeah, you're right. But time will tell. Maybe they're full up and just looking for a parts car."

"Hmmm, maybe. If you're lucky. And luck ain't part of your repertoire of late."

"My luck's gotta change sooner or later. Been bad lately but I used to have great luck… nice wife, two decent kids, a good friend or two. I don't have much luck but what luck I have endures!"

"I still don't see how you're going to get this by Doris."

"Doris who?"

"The Doris who married you and gave you those decent kids."

"Oh her. She's on a need-to-know basis. I'll tell her after the fact. Forgiveness is easier than permission."

"I can see it all now… your tombstone reading 'Here lies Gary Miller. King of idiots."

"Funny, very funny. You're the one who came up with this crazy idea. Maybe you'll be lying next to me in our dirt nap."

"Or not. I have an excuse."

"Oh yeah. What?"

"I'm not Gary Miller. 'nuff said."

"Enough already. I need to do this. Just be sure to be here Saturday morning."

"Well, I was coming over to help you change the oil in Doris' car anyway. Will she be home?"

"Actually no. Your Fred is taking her to his mom's old styling parlor for haircuts."

"Fred didn't tell me. I guess I'm the one on a need-to-know basis."

"Whatever. Just be here."

As Gary hangs up the phone, Doris walks into the room. Gary hurriedly switches to another website to keep the auction site off the screen.

"Good morning, dear. Whatcha got cookin' on the computer already?" asked Doris as she peeked over his shoulder.

"Oh, nothing really. Just checking my email."

"You get email? From whom? You don't like all this new-fangled computer stuff."

"Hey, cut me a break. I know a bit from a byte… I think."

"I suppose so. Did I tell you that I'm heading to the hair stylist with Fred next Saturday? It's his mom's old shop and we're both getting haircuts."

"Yes, you did tell me. This is a platonic relationship, isn't it?"

"Purely. You shouldn't even go there. Fred's harmless and besides Jo keeps him happy as a clam."

"I know, I know. Just kidding." Whispering to himself Gary muttered "Jo just better clam up between now and Saturday."

"What's that?"

"Nothing, nothing. Didn't you just get your hair cut two weeks ago?"

She throws him a frown. "It was *six* weeks ago."

"Really? If you say so. Hey, why not change the style a little? Get a bit funky."

"Funky went out in the '70s. I have an idea though. I hope you'll like it."

"Don't I always like it?"

"It's hard to tell. The last time I called you from the beauty shop you said you loved it without even seeing it!"

"Telepathy. You and I have a metaphysical connection."

"Ooookay, Gary. Whatever you say. Anyway, I need to do the laundry, and you need to get to work on your honey-do list. It's getting late," Doris said as the cuckoo clock began to chirp nine times.

Gary shut down the computer and hoped that next Saturday would be the start of a new adventure and a new lease on his humdrum life.

CHAPTER TEN

The following Saturday morning dawned with sun painting a red glow on the bottom of the cloud layer drifting in from the west. An auspicious start thought Gary to what could become a nerve-racking day. 'Red sky in the morning' didn't apply to computer auctions, did it? The big day had arrived, and he faced it with a bit more trepidation than excitement. The possible outcomes kept playing over and over in his mind... would he win, would he get cold feet, what would he say to Doris? And he had that song 'Little GTO' stuck in his head on a seemingly endless loop. He fixed himself a cup of cinnamon ginger herbal tea, took his vitamins and munched on a slice of sour dough bread slathered with almond butter all with the intent to settle his nerves and boost his energy for the upcoming match. Match? Yeah, he thought, he'd be facing unknown opponents in a struggle of wills and wallets. He certainly had the will, but the wallet was another thing.

The subject GTO had two wheels in the junk yard and the other two on an oily roadway. Not quite a parts car because the engine supposedly ran many years ago or so the description said. As for the rest of the car, it would take thousands of dollars and hundreds of hours to bring it back to drivable condition. Money he didn't have, but the accountant in him rationalized that by spreading the investment over several years he could work into the budget if he worked some overtime, if the washing machine didn't break down and if Doris didn't divorce him. Well, she wouldn't do that, at least he hoped she wouldn't. He'd made some serious financial screwups during their 30-year marriage and she still hung in there. Whatta gal. Thinking of her, she walked into the kitchen happily greeting him.

"Morning dear. You're up and at 'em early today. What gives?"

Uh oh thought Gary. Does she know what I'm up to? Woman's intuition? Did Jo let it slip? A dire sense of paranoia gripped him. Panic clenched his throat.

"Gary? Hello, anyone in there?" Doris asked as she gave him a puzzled look and tapped lightly on his head.

"Huh? Oh, yeah, good morning, Dor. How are you this beautiful morning?" replied Gary.

"I'm fine but you seem a bit more out of it than usual."

"Love you too. I'm ok, just pondering solutions to international conflict and the state of the economy."

"That seems a bit above your pay grade, Gary. Get back down to earth. Speaking of pay, I need a few bucks for my haircut. Got a twenty?" she asked.

"A twenty!! Are you financing your stylist's retirement plan or what?" he remarked.

"That's just for the tip. And I'm not doing any coloring so it's a cheap day."

"I cut my own hair for nothin.'"

"Well, Gary, how do I put this gently. You're folically challenged. And running that skull shaver over your chrome dome doesn't exactly qualify as a haircut. It's more like weed-whacking the desert. No offense."

"I resemble that remark! But you're right as usual. Hey, I turned on the Keurig for you."

"Thanks. I'll drink a cup but then I must run. Fred will be over soon. You remember Fred, the guy across the street with the beautiful head of hair?" she jabbed.

"Thin ice, Alice! Thin ice. Pow, zoom, to the moon!" said Gary stealing a Honeymooner's line.

"So sorry, I couldn't resist. Tell you what. When I get home, I'll bake you some oatmeal cookies."

"Deal. But don't give any to Fred. I want 'em all."

"Ok, my lips are sealed. Speaking of which, give me a kiss I think I hear Fred coming."

"Be good and here's that twenty. Have a fun time."

"You too Gary. Don't do anything stupid and stay out of trouble."

"I'll try my best. Bye."

Doris grabbed her coffee and made for the front door. Gary finished his tea and went to the computer desk and fired up the Dell. A screen shot of some castle in Ireland flashed up and then the login screen. He typed in his code and brought up the car auction site. He was just in time as the auction was about to commence with a few other cars in line before the GTO. Where's Jo, he thought. She's supposed to be here for moral support. He hears the slamming of a hood from the garage. Oh right, she promised to change Doris' oil today returning a favor he'd done for her. Over on the wall, the little cuckoo chirped his unique phrase ten times.

"Yes, thanks for the reminder my little feathered friend. Only a few minutes left before I bid on *my* GTO. It's gonna be a big day for big Gary. Heh Heh Heh" he said aloud while rubbing his hands together. "The '66 Pontiac GTO will soon be mine."

Gary studied the computer screen and decided to enter a pre-bid seconds before the auction started in earnest. Typing in $2500.00 he mumbled "Take that Goat Man. Heh Heh Heh".

The door to the garage opened and Jo walked into the mud room adjoining the kitchen. With a smudge of grease on her cheek, she wore a bandana on her head and was pulling off her work gloves as she called for Gary.

"Hey Gary. Gary? I got the oil changed in the car.

"Hey Jo. How'd that go?"

"The filter was a bear to get at. I almost broke a nail but it's alright. I think we're even now."

Jo pulled open the door to the refrigerator and grabbed a beer from the shelf. In doing so, the can slipped from her hand and bounced on the floor making a loud thud.

"What was that?" Gary asked but wasn't distracted from staring at the computer screen.

"Oh, nothing Gary," she replied and mumbled to herself 'Just a time bomb'.

She replaced the agitated beer can on the shelf and took the only remaining Yuengling. She gently closed the fridge door so as not to disturb the can again and walked over to Gary.

"Hey, help yourself to a beer," said Gary sarcastically.

"Thanks, I already have one," replied Jo as she popped the top.

"Jo, sit. You're just in time. Only five minutes and thirty-eight seconds left in the auction."

Jo pulled up a stool and plopped down next to Gary. She sees the subject GTO on the computer screen which is displaying the current bid.

"So, Gary, how's the bidding going? Is my man Big Gar' winning?"

"Oh baby, I'm high bidder but Goat Man and Chief Pontiac are hot on my trail. Don't people work for a living?"

Jo rolls her eyes and subtly shakes her head wondering what sort of Pandora's box she has opened for Gary.

"For a classic '66 GTO you should be happy all of Detroit isn't in this. I see you're up to $2500."

Just as she said that the bid screen changed.

"Ahh! Goat Man just bid $2550" Gary cried.

Gary frantically starts typing.

"Easy Big Gar'. You have plenty of time. Are you sure you really want this one? I think the Titanic has less rust."

"Rust, schmust. I learned body work in high school. Besides I've got all winter to work on it... with my friends helping me of course," says Gary glancing at Jo.

"Does it even run?" asks Jo.

"I told you that the ad said ran when parked," answered Gary.

"Yeah, well maybe you should be running... away from this."

Gary finishes typing in his next bid and with a wry smile on his face, jabs the enter key only to be interrupted by Jo.

"No! Wait!" shouts Jo.

"What? Why?" answers Gary a bit startled.

"You typed in 26 *thousand* as your maximum bid."

"No, I didn't. It was 2600," replied Gary as he adjusted his glasses.

"I saw three zeros four eyes. Look at the screen!"

On the screen the bid price is rapidly climbing as the

last few seconds of the auction tick off. A constant succession of bids floods the screen with the moniker Big Gar' outbidding everyone. From a slow start of $50 increments the bids are now climbing by hundreds of dollars every few seconds. And Gary knows too well that these auctions are binding contracts. A bead of sweat appears on his brow.

"Looks like you're outbidding everyone automatically."

"Ahhh! I can't afford that much. Doris will kill me. $2800 was my absolute limit," says Gary.

"Hey, listen nimble fingers, I know a loan shark you can call but first we must stop the bleeding. Get into that account screen and cancel your maximum bid… Go!"

"Ok, ok. I just need to delete this…"

"Look Gary, you got an error message," exclaimed Jo.

The computer screen flashes off briefly and then a new screen appears with the message: 'FATAL ERROR. WINDOWS IS SHUTTING DOWN'

"Ahhhhhhh," cries Gary.

"This is going to be not good," utters Jo.

Gary grabs his face in his hands, gets up and sits down at the kitchen table. Jo slides over in front of the computer and tries to reboot it. A few minutes later she has it up and running again. Finding the auction site, she brings up Gary's account and the bid history.

"Ok, Gary. Ready for this?"

"Do I have a choice?" replies Gary.

"Well, I could show Doris, and she could put you out of your misery."

Gary gets up and stands behind Jo and sees the bid history and winning bid.

"Oh... my... God. I think I'm going to be sick," wails Gary. "I need a beer."

"Oh wow, Gary. You won it for ten grand! Look at that bid history! Detroit *did* show up. And they were frantic at the end with that amazing Big Gar' annihilating the field. They never knew what hit 'em!"

"Neither did I," says Gary.

"Hey, I think you should change your username," suggests Jo.

"To what?"

Just then the cuckoo clock chirps 'cuck-oo'.

"CuckooMan! I couldn't have said it better myself," says Jo.

Gary shuffles over to the fridge, opens the door and takes the remaining can of beer.

"Last one," he mumbles as he shuts the door, leans his back against it and goes to pop the tab.

"No Gary. Wait!" exclaims Jo.

Popping the tab, beer sprays out of the previously agitated can and gushes onto the floor. He leans his head back in dejection saying:

"Ohhhh, baby."

CHAPTER ELEVEN

It has been a week since the auction debacle and Gary has yet to tell Doris of his misdeed. It's a Saturday morning and Gary is in the garage with the big door rolled open and is straightening things up, which is usually a spring-cleaning event but now a more pressing need. The GTO is on the way. He has backed Doris' car into the driveway next to his old Honda Ridgeline. The Honda is parked in the driveway because there is barely enough room in the two-car garage for her SUV. The second space is loaded with the ornery lawn mower, sawhorses, boards of various dimensions, various and sundry woodworking tools, a heavy-duty floor jack, old skis, three bikes, boxes of who-knows-what and of course the obligatory corn hole set.

Gary is scratching his head wondering where he's going to put all this stuff. Some, he figures, will be relegated to the basement but he's been loath to lug the bigger tools and boxes down a flight of stairs to join an already crowded room. He thinks that a tarp might work for the lawnmower, and he has a spot for it next to the heat pump unit. There's an Old Town canoe hanging from the rafters which may have to be raised a few inches so as not to bump heads. He's thinking maybe Jo could find room at her place to harbor some of this gear. Regardless it's all got to be moved out this morning because the ETA for the Goat is 1:00 p.m. He loads an old Steppenwolf CD into the dusty player and cranks up the volume a notch as Jo saunters up the driveway sipping on a can of diet soda and munching a cookie.

"She's twenty-eight years old tonight…" sings Gary.

"That's robbin' the cradle for a man of your vintage," chimes Jo as she walks in the open garage door. "So, how's it shakin' big Gar'?"

"Hey Jo, how goes it? That wouldn't be one of Maggie's famous cookies, would it?"

"Yes, and it's the last one. Suffer."

"You're so kind. I'm just straightening up the Gar'-age..get it?"

"Poor, very poor? What did you lose a bet with Doris and cleaning up this mess is your penance?"

"Naw, just makin' some room and pushin' my broom. I need a little extra space for the new addition to the family."

"Really?" asked Jo. "So, the Viagra finally kicked in, huh?"

"Hey, lady. I don't need no stinkin' Viagra."

"And the Pope's a Presbyterian. Besides, aren't you about due for your annual mating ritual?"

"That's semi-annual I'll have you know. I'm still in my prime!"

"Poor guy. My car's oil gets changed more often than that. So, what addition to the family are you referring to?" asks Jo.

"The GTO," replied Gary.

"What?! You said you were going to get out of that deal. That was a week ago. Didn't you call them and explain what happened? That you are dexterously challenged?" asks Jo.

"Thanks for your support, but I did call and no dice," replied Gary.

"But didn't you tell them that you were *the* Gary Miller, of Reading Pennsylvania. Surely your reputation as an idiot preceded you."

"Evidently not. I knew the auction was a binding contract, but I thought they would make an exception. Alas no. The car is mine. End of story."

"And the beginning of your demise. What does Doris think about this?"

"Doris who?" replied Gary.

"Once again, I must remind you. The Doris that does your laundry, cleans your house and, oh, by the way, gave birth to your children. Remember?"

"Oh, her. Ah, no, I didn't tell her."

As Gary said that Jo sprayed the soda she was sipping on all over the floor and bent over laughing.

"Ha ha oh oh,'" Jo coughed. "I, I cccan't believe it."

"I kid you not,'" replied Gary.

"If you're telling me the truth… you're dead. I'd be honored to write your eulogy."

"That's so kind of you. But the queen will obey my commands."

"I repeat," said Jo. "You're dead."

Jo looks around the garage and spies Gary's old compound miter saw on the workbench.

"Hey, can I have your miter saw when your gone?"

"Sure, I mean no. I'm not going anywhere."

"Oh yes you are. To a hot place. A very, very hot place. Gary, I still find this hard to believe. Tell me you're kidding," said Jo.

With that, Gary turns to the cluttered workbench, opens a folder, and hands Jo the receipt for the car.

"You son of a gun. You *did* buy the GTO. And this says it's getting delivered today! Really, Gary, can't I have the miter saw?"

"No! Doris will come around. I hope."

"And how long did you have that Harley Davidson motorcycle back in '96?"

"Five hours. But it was a great five hours!"

"She popped a gasket on that one. You'll never get the Goat in her garage."

"Correction, *my* garage."

"Wasn't that *her* car you rolled out?"

"Yeah."

"And hasn't it been residing here all by its lonesome since purchased?"

"And your point is?"

"Case closed. Bad enough you broke the bank and bought the Goat and now you're kicking her car out to boot?"

"Hey, you saw a picture of the car. I need all this space to work on it. My own fixer-upper!"

"The mortician will have a fixer-upper… You! Ain't gonna happen my man. No way two cars are going to fit in here. The Hog fit, barely, even if it was for only five hours."

"Stop reminding me of the Harley. But you're wrong. Her car will have to stay outside. I'll need this space and more. Car here, parts there. The rest of the workbench is under this pile somewhere."

"And your casket will look nice right here under the canoe. Gary, I cannot fathom that you are getting the Goat."

"Fathom this. You know I've been talking about one for years. It's my all-time favorite. Don't you remember that I told you that my dad had one just like it. In fact, I drove it on my first real date with Doris."

"That story I remember. It could have been your *last* date with her. You totaled the car the same night, didn't you?"

"Almost. We were horsing around with the radio, and she grabbed my hand and gave it friendly bite. Then I kind of lost control of the car when that buck jumped out of the woods," said Gary.

"Love at first bite!" remarked Jo.

"Yeah, luckily we were not injured. We never found that jeweled necklace she was wearing though. Well, what was left of the car was sold to a body shop. I think we coulda fixed it."

"I can't believe she married you after you almost killed her."

"I should kill you for teaching me about that auction website!"

"Most users are adept, not inept like Big Gar', king of the keyboard."

"It's Doris's fault actually. She bought me the darn computer."

"Oh, don't say that to her or you'll be dead twice."

"You can't be dead twice!"

"An exception will be made for the king of idiots."

"Jo, you gotta help me gal. The car is coming, and I haven't slept a wink all week trying to think of a way to tell Doris. I'm just working out here trying to avoid her. What would you do?"

"Bequeath my miter saw to my best friend."

"Listen, help me find a way out of this and I'll gladly give you the damn saw and throw in a fishing rod too! I'm desperate."

"Hmmm," pondered Jo, "I'm fresh out of lies, been a busy week. Maybe Burt will have an idea. He's been in and out of a lot of jams," said Jo.

"Yeah! Run over there and drag him here!"

"What will I say to him?" asked Jo as she headed out the door.

"He's been drooling over that canoe for years. If he rescues me, tell him it's his!"

"And I still get the miter saw?" Jo asked over her shoulder as she ran out the door.

Gary picks up a whiffle ball and chucks it at Jo, just missing her head.

CHAPTER TWELVE

Meanwhile in the kitchen, Doris is hurriedly baking a pie while Gary, she thought, was just tinkering in the garage. The kitchen in the Miller household was primarily Doris's domain. She'd picked out the knotty hickory cabinets when they did the remodel ten years ago. Gary had the job of removing the old ones and hanging the new ones. They'd gotten the deal of a lifetime which was the only reason they'd decided to remodel. A friend was a photographer for a company that did all those pictures seen in the home building magazines. In this instance, a kitchen cabinet maker shipped an entire set to the warehouse where photos were taken which was how the game was played. Usually, the cabinets were returned after the shooting, but this manufacturer, being a long distance away, said to just keep them in return for the pictures. The friend mentioned that the cabinets were now for sale. Gary and Doris went to the warehouse, loved the cabinets, and were floored by the price… $5000 for the entire kitchen. Gary couldn't reach for his wallet quickly enough, but in fact, he wrote a check against his home equity account and the project was on.

Doris of course put her own touch on the decorations which included a Florentine tile backsplash with a few handmade tiles picturing local waterfowl, a shelf which held her collection of a dozen German beer steins, and a plaque that read 'Doris's kitchen' which Gary had bought her for her birthday. Though not the sharpest knife in the drawer, Gary did have an instinct for pleasing Doris. And the way he stumbled through life and marriage, he figured that he needed all the brownie points he could collect.

But today she was pressed for time because she, Maggie, and Fred were going to see Maggie's granddaughter's dance recital and must not be a minute late. Dusting himself off, Gary entered the kitchen.

"Hi, honey. Didn't know you were up," remarked Gary.

"I've been up for two hours so I thought I'd bake a pie. Someone's been banging around in the garage," she replied.

"Oops! I forgot that you could hear that up in the bedroom. Was I making that much noise?"

"You could have woken the dead."

"My soon to be comrades," Gary muttered to himself.

"Say what?" Doris asked as she intently crimped the edges of a pie crust.

"Nothing, nothing. Anyway, good morning and sorry I woke you."

Turning to Gary with her doughy hands held back, she gives Gary a kiss.

"It's okay. I was awake anyway. I'm just happy that you've finally started to clean up the garage. Oooh! You're really dirty… and smelly!"

"And I love you too. Don't my pheromones turn you on?" Gary asks when he goes to hug her.

Shying away she says "And I love you. Pheromones and whatever else you are excreting… I guess."

Waving her hand in front of her nose, she goes back to crimping the pie.

"What kind of pie is that?" asks Gary.

"Apple and no you can't have any when it's done. Everyone's coming over tomorrow night to play cards, so I thought I'd make some dessert. Burt loves my apple pie!"

"So do I," says Gary. "Don't I count?"

"Of course you do dear. Just not today. You'll have to wait until then for a slice."

"And after dessert, then what?" Gary snickered and gave her a wink.

"Maybe I'll check out your pheromones."

"Do I have to shower?"

Gary ducked the piece of dough tossed in his direction.

"Take your chances and see. Hey, do something useful while in my kitchen. Open the oven door so I can put this pie in."

"So, this is *your* kitchen?" Gary quizzed.

Doris nods toward a plaque on the wall hanging proudly above the spice rack.

"Yep. Says so right there on that plaque you gave me for my birthday last year… Doris's Kitchen."

"Just checking. Hey, I need to tell you something important. I…" starts Gary but he's abruptly cut off.

"Ohhh, look at the time! Gary, you'll have to take the pie out of the oven when it's done. Can you remember to do that? I mean you *must* remember to do that," she said emphatically.

"Let's see. Take pie 'A' out of oven 'B' and place it on counter 'C'. Is that right?"

"Yes, that's correct. And if you forget, you'll be dead 'D'.

"That will be the third time today but who's counting?"

"What are you talking about?"

"Look honey, I've been wanting to tell you something. A couple of days ago I accidently..,"

She cuts him off again when the doorbell rings.

"That's the gang now. I've got to go dear. You can tell me later. Can you clean up the kitchen?"

"*Your* kitchen?" Gary asks.

"Of course. And try not to touch anything with those clothes. You're a mess."

"And stinky too. How's this, I'll use my tongue," says Gary as he sticks out his tongue and goes to lick the countertop.

"You're disgusting," Doris frowns.

"Thank you," replies Gary as Fred enters the kitchen with Maggie close behind.

"We let ourselves in," says Fred. "Come on Doris, we'll be late. Oh, hi there. I guess that's you Gary under all that grime."

"Grime pays. Hey Maggie, did you bring any cookies? Jo's already tortured me this morning by eating one and not sharing."

"No, I'm sorry. I really meant to give you some but aside from a few I gave to Jo, Burt finished off the whole batch last night."

"Scratch the canoe," Gary mumbled.

"What do you mean, dear?" asked Maggie. "Oh, never mind. We must run, Doris. We cannot be late for the recital."

"Bye dear," says Doris as she hurries by Gary blowing him a kiss. "And don't forget my pie!"

"*Our* pie!" Gary corrected. "Maggie, she threatened me with death if I forget to take it out of the oven."

"Doris, how could you do that to my Gary. Why I would only spank him," proffers Maggie.

"See honey. She loves me more than you do!"

"We'll see about that later Mr. Pheromones."

Doris throws Gary a wink and a coy smile and out the door the three of them go.

"I wonder if dead guys get lucky?" Gary muses as he starts wiping down the countertop.

CHAPTER THIRTEEN

After finishing up in the kitchen, Gary heads back to the garage and continues to clean up 'his' side by relocating various machines and tools. The odd pieces of 2x4s that were left over from various projects and the cove molding remnants from the kitchen remodel are relegated to the bed of his pickup truck for a trip to the dump. Anything that he hasn't used in five years is added to the pile though it pains him to chuck anything that he may have a use for at some point in his lifetime. Steel yourself, he mutters. The car project trumps all this assorted junk so let it go. Focus on the task at hand.

And now that Doris has gone, he jumps in her car and goes to start it but looks in the rearview mirror and sees Jo and Burt walking up the driveway. Getting out, he's beaming.

"Good goin', Jo. You found Burt," says Gary.

"Can I have the paddles along with the canoe?" asks Burt.

"I'm getting his miter saw," says Jo.

"Wait a minute. Nobody gets nothin' until you come up with a plan to explain this to Doris. Burt, didn't Jo tell you my problem?"

"Sure she did. As I see it, you're dead regardless. What about the life vests?" says Burt.

"Are there any more blades for the saw?" chimes in Jo.

"Come on you thieves. I'm hurtin' here. I need to know what to do."

"Tell her the truth," advises Burt.

"And I'll get the consequences. She'll kill me. No. No way."

Burt is rubbing his chin with a quizzical look in his eye.

"Ok, but first you have to help *me*," says Burt. "I have a moral dilemma. See, if you die, Doris will probably give me the canoe. If I rescue you, I get the canoe. So either way, I get the canoe. Therefore, you'll have to up the ante a bit to resolve my dilemma. How about those golf clubs?" says Burt.

"Interesting," says Gary. "A moral dilemma that includes *blackmail!* Okay, Okay. Take the whole garage. What should I do?"

"What part of 'truth' don't you understand, lamebrain?" quips Jo.

"The truth part," answers Gary.

"Look Gary," says Burt. "Canoe and golf clubs aside, you and Doris have been married for twenty-some years, right? You've had your ups and downs like everyone else. Well, then this too shall pass."

"Yeah, like when I accidentally threw out Fred's autographed Yankee's hat last year. He was steamed but eventually got over it," says Jo.

"In three months and a Rolex watch later," recalls Burt.

"Fauxlex. Got it on the street in New York City," replied Jo.

"A frankenwatch, hmmm? I won't tell him if you give me your miter saw," says Burt.

"And out the window goes the last piece of Burt's morality!" laughs Jo.

All heads turn toward the street at the sound of air brakes on a roll back truck as it stops in front of the house. And on its carrying bed sits a somewhat forlorn automobile that has seen better days... much better. Of course, it's Gary's GTO. Their faces are aghast to behold the sight of it. The truck driver dismounts and walks up the driveway.

"It's here!" says Gary. "My coffin, er, my car. Help me get Doris's car out of here. Jo, you get in it and back it out onto the street while I meet the driver. Burt, you keep thinkin'."

"The junk yard is about two miles down the road. Take a left on Main Street," quips Burt to the truck driver.

"My thoughts exactly," he replies. "But my bill of lading indicates 105 Meadow St., Reading, PA. And this is Meadow Street and the number on the door says 105. I think I got it right. Who's the proud owner?"

"That'd be me," says Gary. "Where do I sign?"

"On the dotted line... if you dare," says the driver. "For fifty bucks, I'd be happy to drop it at the junk yard."

"Nah," replies Gary. "I'm... we're gonna fix it up."

"Hmmm. Lemme guess," says the driver. "That nice car there belongs to the wife and she's not around right now. By the look on your face, she doesn't know about the rust bucket, do she?"

"You should practice ESP," says Gary. "Receipt please."

The truck driver gives Gary a copy of the receipt and goes to work unloading the GTO.

"How'd he know?" asks Gary.

"It's the look of fear and apprehension that you are displaying. You're an open book," says Burt.

"Well, open or not, it's here. Let's get at it," says Gary.

With Doris's car now parked on the street, the GTO is dragged off the truck and Gary, Burt and Jo slowly muscle it up the driveway and into the now vacant space in the garage. The car is pretty beaten up with one door a different color, a half flat tire, a missing hub cap and spots of primer and rust everywhere. Gary, though apprehensive, is now beaming like a proud father.

"Isn't she great?" proses Gary. "Even better than the pictures we'd seen. I can just imagine what she'll look like a year from now... Big tires, racing stripes, the works!"

"I didn't know Rustoleum built cars," cracks Burt. "Reality check, Gary. You still have the Doris problem."

"Oh, yeah. Thanks for busting my bubble, Burt."

"No sweat. That's what I'm here for. So, what *are* you going to say to Doris?"

"Look what followed me home, dear. That's it! I'll buy her another puppy like when we got Nicky. She wouldn't kill me then. Oh, the heck with it. Let's see if this baby starts. I'll worry about Doris later."

They pop the hood and see that most of the big pieces are there and seem to be connected just like in the pictures from the auction. They check the oil and it's full, albeit a bit dirty looking. Jo pulls a spark plug and finding it acceptably clean, replaces it and checks the connections on the other seven plugs. Hooking up a charger to the battery, Gary climbs in the car and turns the key one click to the 'on' position.

"We got idiot lights!" exclaims Gary.

"An idiot would know," says Burt. "Turn it to start."

The engine actually cranks for a few seconds which gets smiles and nods from the guys but doesn't start. He tries again but the same result. Jo unscrews the wing nut and takes off the rust-pitted chrome air cleaner. She grabs a spray can of starting fluid and gives the carburetor a shot.

"Hold it Gary while Jo sprays the starting fluid. We don't need to singe her hairdo with a backfire," says Burt. "Ok, she's clear, now give it a go."

Gary cranks the engine again, but again it doesn't start.

"The owner from Pittsburgh said he had it running recently," says Gary.

"Maybe it only runs in Pittsburgh," says Jo.

"Gary, pump the gas pedal and hold it to the floor. Jo, give it another shot of fluid," directs Burt.

Jo again sprays the carburetor's throat and gives Gary a thumbs up. A few cranks later the engine springs to life, belches a cloud of black smoke but settles into a rumbling idle.

"Hurray!" they shout in unison.

"Sounds great Gary," says Jo.

"Not bad. Not bad at all," says a surprised Burt.

Gary gets out of the car, and they all stand around the engine bay peering in.

"Nothin' sounds like a GTO with those cool mufflers. This is a great day my friends!" says Gary.

As they ponder the car, Doris and Fred are walking up the driveway and into the garage. The guys don't notice them.

"Whose car is that, Gary?" asks Doris.

Surprised, Gary, Jo and Burt turn to Doris with their mouths agape. Gary starts to ramble as Jo and Burt take a step back.

"Oh, hhhhi, dear. I didn't expect you home so soon. How was the recital? I'l bet…"

"Jo, what's going on?" interrupts Doris. "I know something's up. And why is my car out in the street?"

"Uh, er, uh, I ah, well…"

"Better fess up Gary," says Burt.

"Fess up to what?" asks Doris.

"IwaslookingforaGTOandbidforoneontheinternetandmadeamistakeandendeduppayingtenthousanddollarsforitandhereitis. Do you like it?"

"You what?!!!" exclaimed Doris. "Ten thousand dollars!"

Doris has her hands on her hips and with a reddening face throws Gary an icy stare. The GTO's engine dies, a tire hisses flat, and a headlamp falls off hanging by its wire.

"That stare killed the car. I guess you're next," says Jo.

"Listen Dor baby. I can explain. I really wanted to tell you, but I was too embarrassed. And I tried to tell you this morning, but you wouldn't let me."

"Get that car out and our money back before I…"

"Here it comes," says Burt.

Burt and Jo turn away and try to slink out the garage door.

"Not so fast there," says Fred. "Get back here. I think I smell a conspiracy."

"Jo and I are just innocent bystanders, Doris," says Burt. "Honest. We just found out about this stupid, foolhardy, dastardly scheme this morning."

"No canoe for you," Gary says to Burt.

Doris puts her hands to her face and begins to cry.

"Jesus mini, Gary! We skimp and scrape to save money and you blow it on some… bag of rust with three and half tires! What about me, Gary? Don't I have a say here?"

Gary walks over to Doris and puts his arm around her waist.

"I'm sorry. Really. I didn't mean not to tell you. But it was an accident. I pushed the wrong button on the computer and it just… happened. Besides you bought me that stupid computer…"

Jo stifles a fake cough and shakes her head no.

"Oh, yeah, right," says Gary. "What I meant to say was that I thought it would be nice to have a car like the one we had our first date in. We could fix it up and do cruise nights together. After all, the kids are away at school, and it might be fun to get out of the house a bit. Just like old times."

"Exactly like old times! We didn't have any money then either! Now we don't even have enough to put gas in it."

"Doris could steer, and you could push," Jo quips.

Doris gives Jo the look which knocks her a step backwards.

"Shut up Jo and avoid eye contact," says Burt.

"Gary, you've had some real screw ups, but this takes the cake" says Doris.

"Speaking of cake, do I smell apples burning?" asks Fred.

"Uh oh," says Gary.

"My pie!" shouts Doris.

They all run to the kitchen door as a slight stream of smoke drifts into the garage.

CHAPTER FOURTEEN

They're all standing around the kitchen island staring at the charred crust of the pie which Doris had plucked from the oven. It was still oozing its contents of apple, sugar and cinnamon. The window is open to allow fresh air to replace the haze that the cooktop fan is slowly exhausting. Burt's wife Maggie has shown up and is holding a handkerchief to her face which does little to filter the acrid smoke. Doris stands stoically by with her arms folded and shaking her head slowly from side to side. She casts a dejected look in Gary's direction. Gary is picking at the pie with a fork, peeling back the crust in sections and checking out the pie's innards.

"You know, I bet the inside is still good," quips Gary.

"Have at it, Chef Burn-ar-dee!" answers Doris.

"I said I was sorry."

"You're beginning to sound like a broken record today."

"By the way, thanks for not killing me."

"Day's not over," says Doris.

"I'll kill him for the canoe!" chimes in Burt.

"I'll…"

"No miter saw for you, Jo! You guys are freaking me out."

"Ten thousand dollars for that car freaks me out," says Doris.

"Okay, I'm an idiot," admits Gary.

"I'll second that," says Jo.

"All in favor?" Burt asks.

"Aye!" they all reply.

"If elected I will not serve," says Gary.

"Too late. All hail the king of idiots," says Jo.

"Hail!" they shouted.

"Okay, okay my royal subjects. Want me to fall on my sword?"

"No. That will void your life insurance. Allow me," offers Doris.

Gary takes a forkful of filling from the steaming pie, blows on it and takes a nibble. Nodding his head and licking his lips he mouths the piece remaining on his fork.

"Mmmm… MacIntosh with a hint of cinnamon and a uh… charcoal finish."

"Always the comedian," says Jo.

"Hey, Dor. Look at it this way. The ten grand is just in a different form. It went from being mere numbers on an account page to a tangible asset!"

"Great, now you're an accountant. And where are you going to get the money to fix it up? Oh, I know. You can sell stock as 'Gary's Garage, Incorporated'. Their motto: 'Where stupidity meets reality'."

"But honey. It's a GTO, a Goat. Don't you remember?"

"Gary, I don't care if it has four legs or four wheels. The car goes, and you are confined to the garage until it does!"

"You have a point, dear," injects Maggie. "Every evening and weekend in the garage until the car is re-sold. And since Burt had a hand in this plot, he can help until Gary gets rid of it. At least we'll know where they are and not out gallivanting around all over the place."

"Right" agrees Doris. "No canoeing or fishing or golfing. You know how that leads to trouble."

"But that's house arrest. It's cruel not to mention unusual," says Gary.

"Beats the death penalty that you narrowly avoided… so far," says Doris.

"Well guys," remarks Jo. "Been nice knowin' ya. See ya in a year or two."

Jo rubs her hands together and turns to leave.

"Hold on there, bucko," orders Burt. "I have one word for you."

"What?"

"Do da term Fauxlex strike a familiar note?"

Jo's eyes go wide, shakes her head no to Burt and plops down on a kitchen stool avoiding Fred's questioning stare after he glances at his ostentatious wristwatch.

CHAPTER FIFTEEN

Later that afternoon, Gary, Jo and Burt are mulling their fate in the garage to which they've been sequestered. Gary is still admiring the Goat and Jo seems to have accepted her fate as she finds a rag and starts polishing the chrome air cleaner. Burt is fumbling with the hanging headlight and is trying to maneuver it back into its place.

"Look at the bright side, buddies," says Gary. "We can order pizza and beer and listen to ball games on the radio while we work. We'll shine up the GTO a bit, put her back up for sale and be out of here in a week or two."

"I wanna see da warden," says Jo.

"My tee time was an hour ago. I'm already having golf withdrawals," says Burt.

"This is just a different form of bonding among friends!" says Gary.

"I'd like to bond a wrench with your face," said Burt.

"Burt, you can go bond with yourself. There are some Victoria's Secret catalogues in the recyclables."

"Really?" asks Jo. "I've been wondering who's been robbing my mail. But, hey, that's what we need! We can put team posters on the walls and a few pinups too. I'll get one of Arnold Schwartzeneger in a speedo.

"No!" Gary and Burt shout in unison.

"But, hey, Jo does have a point there. Why not have some fun while we can? We'll turn this garage into a den of iniquity… unisex of course," says Gary bowing to Jo. "Yeah, we'll show 'em. But we need a few iniquinettes!"

"I can make a few calls," says Jo rubbing her chin in a pensive gaze.

"Whoa, there. Wait a minute Lone Ranger and Pocahontas," interrupts Burt. "Check your hormones at the door. Gary, you're lucky to be among the living right now. Jo can get away with it because she's… well, challenged. Let's not push our luck."

"Once again, oh wise one, you are correct. Let's wait until they at least leave the kitchen. In the meantime, why don't we start to clean up the interior of the Goat. I can bring in the portable and we can watch the ballgame on TV. Free beer for all!"

"Hail, King Gary!" says Burt.

"Here, here!" says Jo. "All this planning makes me hungry. I could use some pizza. I know the manager over at Hoot Owl Pizza which has some fine delivery gals that you boys might like!" says Jo.

"A woman after my own heart," says Gary. "Doris would never do that."

"Wives don't," says Burt. "That's what we have Jo for."

"Just doin' my part to help the team. It'll be the Chippendales next week!" says Jo.

"Or not," remarks Burt. "When the gals arrive, I'll be the designated looker."

"That could be dangerous for a man of your age," says Gary. "Looking at women who are under the age of thirty can cause cataracts."

"Heck, Burt has hemorrhoids older that that!" cracks Jo.

"And proud of 'em," says Burt.

With that, the inmates are invigorated by their new mission to make the garage into a man-cum-gal cave. Gary puts a few more cans of beer into the mini fridge, Burt finds an extension cord for the TV and Jo dials away for a few pizzas. What could possibly go wrong?

CHAPTER SIXTEEN

Later that evening the garage is looking a lot better now that the gang has found a new mission. The floor has been mopped clean except for a few recalcitrant oil stains. There is room for the GTO, a worktable, an old wooden rocking chair with a big hole in its cane seat and a metal folding tray table for the TV. Jo has gotten the flat tire off the Goat and the left rear is up on a jack stand. Burt has donated a few pinups that adorn the wall. They were, not surprisingly, printed by the Ridgid Tool Company and date from the 1960s. He thought that it would make the GTO feel more at home. Jo wanted one of the Chippendales, but that idea was vetoed. But as a concession, Gary found an old unused picture frame with a stock photo of some handsome dude. Jo thought it would do temporarily being better than nothing. Gary has dusted off two old vinyl-woven lawn chairs which, along with the rocker, face the TV. He has adjusted the rabbit ears antenna to tune in a college football game. It's the fourth quarter and the score had been tied but the commentator has just announced a touchdown.

"Hurray Penn State!" shout Gary and Burt.

"The receiver pushed my defender. Where's the flag?" asks Jo.

"In the ref's pocket where it belongs," says Gary. "Six points closer to you paying up!"

"That's an offensive penalty!" says Jo who had the misfortune of graduating from the opposing team's school.

"Your whole team is offensive... they stink!" jokes Gary who high fives Burt.

"Man, what a game. Except for that last TD, they do have a good defense," chimes in Burt.

"Not good enough when the ref is on your side," replies Jo. "He should be wearing a blue uniform like your team."

"There're still a few minutes left for your guys to score. We'll see if they can come back."

"Yeah, the fat lady hasn't sung yet," says Jo.

"No, she's still playing center for your team!" quips Burt high fiving Gary again.

"Right arm, brother! Hooowee, what a game," says Gary. "Hey, I've worked up an appetite. Shouldn't that pizza be here soon?"

"Yeah, and more beer too!" says Jo. "I've requested that hotties Brenda and Bonnie deliver it. Burt might like that if he can handle it."

"Glasses, check. Pacemaker on stun, check. Libido engaged, check. All systems go," he replies.

"Just don't blast off all over my garage, Captain Kirk," orders Gary.

Then there is a 'knock, knock' voiced behind them at the open garage door. Two hot-looking delivery gals wearing short shorts peak into the garage. Each is holding a pizza box in front of them just below their cleavage-revealing tank tops. The guys turn to look, and Burt's jaw is hanging open. Jo chuckles and winks at the girls.

"Pizza's here. Buckle up Burt!" says Jo.

"Enter at your own risk ladies," says Gary.

"Oh, you guys look pretty harmless. At least that is what Jo tells us," Brenda remarks.

"Hi Brenda. Hi Bonnie. Keep your eye on that old one though," Jo nods to Burt. "He's bionic."

"Oh yeah? Which parts?" Bonnie coyly asks, throwing a smile Burt's way.

"Abub, ahh, uhh," Burt stutters.

"That's Romulan for abub, ahh, uh," Gary says.

"Romulan? You guys Trekkies?" Brenda asks.

"Original Trekkies. Saw the very first episode when it hit the airwaves," Gary offered.

"Wow, you don't look that old," says Bonnie throwing another smile at Burt.

"Abub, ahh, uhh," he utters.

"That's some vocabulary you have there," says Bonnie. "I wish I knew Romulan, but they didn't offer it in high school."

"Your loss," Brenda says. "Hey, is that a '66 GTO? Wow, who's car?"

"It belongs to the guy who's paying for the pizza," Jo answers.

"Do you know GTOs?" Gary asks.

"A little. My ex-boyfriend had one just like it, only… well, nicer. Actually, I helped him work on it on occasion. Looks like this one has that high output 389. I got good at tune ups if you need some advice. We also changed the gear ratio on the rear end."

Gary and Burt are now staring at each other in disbelief thinking they have died and gone to heaven.

"Really?" Gary quizzes. "Well, maybe you can tell me a little more about your rear end, er, the car's rear end."

"Cost you a slice of pizza," Brenda demands.

Looking at Burt, Gary asks "Does it get any better than this, man?"

Just then, there is a noise at the open garage door. A beautiful blonde dressed in jeans, a too tight white blouse and pushing a hand cart loaded with three cases of Yuengling lager rolls into the garage.

"That answers my own question," says Gary.

"Abub, ahh, uhh," Burt garbles shaking his head and slouching in the lawn chair fanning himself.

Eventually the testosterone subsides, and they all grab a slice of pizza and pop beers. Jo formally introduces all the girls, and they start talking about the football game which Penn State has won. Gloria, the beer gal, mentions she had to quit football cheerleading due to her big bouncing boobs which hurt too much and distracted the football players. Burt, now speechless with that remark, looks up to heaven and silently lips 'thank you.'

CHAPTER SEVENTEEN

Gary's garage has taken a decidedly different turn. From a tangled mess of household equipment and debris with just enough room for Doris's car, it has become a mancave haven… car, football, beer and hot women… just like in the movies. Gary and Brenda are bent over the front of the engine compartment tinkering with the carburetor with just their backsides visible to the others. Burt and Bonnie have plopped into the lawn chairs and are watching another football game. Bonnie has taken him under her wing and is feeding him bites of pizza. When his eyes shift to Brenda's shapely rear end, she asks him if he speaks French.

"Parlez vous Francais, Burt?" she asks.

Having somewhat reclaimed his senses he replies.

"Nein, Ich kann nicht," he utters in basic German.

"So, I guess 'manage a trois' is lost on you?"

Well, *that* he understands and reverts to mindlessness and Romulan.

"Abub, ahh, uhh."

"Here, take another bite."

Jo has cozied into the rocker after placing a cushion over the hole and with a beer in one hand and a slice in the other, she is mumbling encouragement to her pick on the game. They're still behind but it's another close game.

But then the party is interrupted as the door to the kitchen opens and in walk Doris and Maggie. They are dumbfounded at the scene before them, and Jo sees them first.

"Guys, I just remembered that I have a dentist appointment. I gotta scram," she says.

From under the hood without looking up, Gary replies.

"It's Saturday night. No dentist is working."

Gary looks over and sees Doris, straightens up and bangs his head on the hood.

"Ow.Hhhi,dear.Justtunin'upthecarandgettingsometi psfromBrendawhoisreallyverygood.."

"Looks like you were wrong, Maggie. Trouble is just starting for this crew," Doris grits.

"So I see. What do you have to say for yourself, Burt?" she adds.

"Abub, ahh, uhh."

"I think that's Romulan," Bonnie says offering him another bite of pizza.

"Houston, we have a problem," Jo interjects.

"Not Houston. It's Gary that has a problem," Doris says.

"And Burt too from the looks of it," adds Maggie.

"Dor, baby, it's not what it looks like," says Gary.

"And what *does* it look like?" she questions.

"Like you gonna die yet today," Jo quips.

"Dang, she was right. Day ain't over," says Gary.

"Ladies, look. It was my fault," confesses Jo. "I thought it would be nice to, you know, celebrate the new car. Like the pinups? My Chippendales were vetoed."

"Lovely pinups. Especially the live ones. Enjoying your pizza, Burt?" Maggie asks.

"Abub, ahh, uhh."

Glancing at Doris, Maggie says "He gets that way whenever beautiful young women are around. It was two weeks before he could tell me his name when we first met."

"Well, Gary, name your poison," Doris commands.

"Jo's tellin' the truth, Dor. Burt and I are just innocent stand by hers, er, bystanders."

"You can't even spell innocent."

Brenda puts down the wrench she was holding and takes off the work gloves Gary had provided. Wiping a long curl from her face she addresses Doris.

"Well, we better be getting back to work. For what it's worth, we're Jo's cousins. Come on, Bonnie and Gloria, let's hit it. Bye everyone!"

The girls exit through the garage door and all eyes follow them. Doris is shaking her head and has her hands on her hips. Gary looks at her and envisions steam rising from her new hairdo.

"There, ya see, Dor. Just a little of Jo's frivolity."

"Yeah, no harm done. We're just tryin' to kid around with Burt."

"So, what do *you* have to say for yourself?" Maggie asks Burt.

"I temporarily plead insanity."

Gary goes over to Burt and gives him a one-armed hug.

"And I thought the delivery ladies would be too much for you."

"I only had one eye open." Burt suggests. "When you get to be my age, you have to learn how to pace yourself."

Doris has had enough and turns on her heel heading to the kitchen. Passing Gary, she grabs his beer, his slice of pizza and retires into the kitchen slamming the door behind her.

CHAPTER EIGHTEEN

A week has passed… a long week. Doris was giving him the silent treatment for the most part but did respond to his questions albeit in an abbreviated clip. As much as he disliked his job, it did become a respite from the tension at home. And it was inventory week, the lowest rung on his top ten gripes of being the manager. But then he thought 'there are worse fates' and hunkered down over boxes of Nikes and commenced with the counting. At least the task got his mind off the crisis at home.

Handing off the tedious counting to one of his coworkers freed his creative mind to ponder a plan to resolve the GTO issue. 'Where there's a will, there's a way' seemed to be his current mantra. But just how could he convince Doris to see the error of her ways… his error, her ways. Give it time, he thought, and she'll come around. But how much time would it take and what could he do in the meantime? Well, he'd start the restoration a little at a time to enhance the car's value if it did come down to selling it. Or better case, he'd convince her that it truly was an investment and worth keeping.

The entire week passed with no give on Doris's part. The ads Gary had placed on a few car websites were getting hits, much to his dismay. He winced every time an inquiring email arrived in his account, and he dragged his feet in responding. As Friday night came around, he plunged in and started to remove the carburetor from the engine. He first took a picture on his phone just to be sure he could reassemble it later. There weren't too many hoses and mechanical connections to deal with since the car was forty years old. Back then you could actually work on cars without being a computer scientist. He undid the bolts holding the carb to the intake manifold, deftly removed it to the workbench and sat it on an old aluminum baking tray. Spraying it with a dripping coat of auto parts cleaner and donning rubber gloves, he started at it with an old toothbrush and a rag. An hour later he'd not made much progress as the grime was caked on, and it was hard to get into all the little nooks and crannies. Enough for now, he thought. Maybe Jo would have a better idea. He wiped off the excess cleaner and put it in a cardboard box for safekeeping.

Saturday morning was a little more pleasant with him making breakfast for Doris, which she reluctantly ate but enjoyed and succinctly thanked him. She had a few chores to do and left Gary sitting at the computer wearing earbuds and eating a bowl of oatmeal. He's softly singing along with Patsy Cline's 'Crazy'. He doesn't see Jo walk in from the garage, open the fridge and grab a beer. The 'pop' startles Gary and he turns to Jo.

"A knock would have sufficed!"

"Since when do I ever knock?" answers Jo.

"Since now. Why don't you grab a beer while you're at it?"

"Yet again, I already have one!" Jo replies taking a swig. "Ahhh, nothing like that first beer o' the day."

"It's only nine a.m. Jo."

"Shhh… don't tell the beer. Gimme a break, it's Saturday man."

"Tell that to your liver."

"My liver is lovely. In fact, I just got a clean bill of health from my gynecologist. "

"She checks livers?"

"Not really, but it's all connected one way or another. So, anyway Gar', whacha doin' on the computer that got you into trouble. You a glutton for punishment?"

"Ancient history, my friend. Time and tide stop for no man. Onward we march. I'm looking for a carburetor rebuild kit for the GTO."

"The carb sitting on that engine out there is the heart of the entire machine with lots of precision parts and adjustments. Why don't you start on something simple like a fender? A dumb piece like that would be perfect for the likes of you."

"So you say. Besides, the aforementioned carburetor in now sitting in that box over there on the floor."

She goes over to the box, looks in and gasps.

"Wha… What did you do?" Jo stammers clutching her chest. "You..You deflowered the Goat!"

"I don't think 'deflowered' is the appropriate word," Gary says.

"Works for me. And now you've thrown it in a cruddy cardboard box? Disgraceful!"

"Jo, you understand it's just a carb."

"Just a carb you say? Gar', this is the holy grail of carburetors… A Carter AFB four barrel. An icon of the '60s. You don't just rip it off and throw it in a box. That's sacrilegious… hell awaits you!"

"Nah, I think St. Peter is into carbs. He'd let me in, being a car guy."

"Good thing. Well, I'm here to help you out of this mess before you really screw up again."

"Your moral support is unfathomable. The first thing I need to do is to clean it up. What would I use to clean a carb, Jo?"

"Carb cleaner."

"Really? How logical."

"That's why you need me. Always thinkin'."

"If your nose was working you could smell the carb cleaner I've already used. I mean *really* clean… showroom clean. Carb cleaner only gets you so far. I can't seem to get into the tight places."

"Well, then you need lots more elbow grease or high-pressure water to blast it off. Nothing else will do."

The sound of feet walking brings Doris into the kitchen. She eyes the two rascals with suspicion but puts on a friendly face.

"Good morning, Jo. Drinkin' your breakfast, I see," Doris remarks.

"It's nine o'clock somewhere!" Jo responds.

"Don't you mean five o'clock?" Doris asks.

"Dor, don't get her started. She's already flustered knowing I removed the carburetor from the GTO."

"How are you going to sell it without a carburetor?" Doris asks.

"It'll go back on when it's cleaned up. And it should run better too. Any prospective buyers will appreciate that," Gary adds. "Besides, we need something to do while in jail."

"What's that smell?"

"Carb cleaner. Sorry, I'll take it back out to the shop in a minute."

Doris heads for the dishwasher and starts to unload it. The Maytag is relatively new and has lots of new-fangled buttons and electronic displays. It even chimes when it's done its job.

"Oooh, I'm jealous," Jo says. "A high-tech machine you got there Doris. New one, huh?"

"Yes, nice, isn't it?" Gary bought it for my birthday... back a month ago when we had money. It's what every woman wants," Doris says rolling her eyes.

"He's a different sort isn't he... but you know that," Jo says.

"Don't I."

"I asked you what you wanted..." Gary starts to say.

"Zip it. Don't you ever learn?" Jo questions.

"Well, it *is* nice," Doris admitted. "It's quiet and scrubs things like new. The heavy-duty cycle blasted the burnt crust right off the infamous pie pan. Look!"

"Hey, isn't that the one Gary left smoldering in the oven?" Jo asks.

"One and the same. I thought I might have to chuck it but here it is, spic and span."

That comment engaged a deep recess in Gary's brain where a technical problem was bouncing around. Could the dishwasher? ...hmmm.

"Oh, I'm late again," Doris continued. "Finish this for me Gary, will you? I gotta run to do the food shopping."

"No problem. Jo, go earn your beer."

"Happy to help Doris any day," Jo said. "I know where everything goes being this is my home away from home."

"Ok, thanks Jo. Bye guys. Be good... I know that is asking a lot but try... please!"

"Ok honey. We'll be good. Scouts honor," Gary said holding up his hand in the Boy Scout salute.

The moment she leaves, Gary and Jo amble over to the dishwasher and stare at it in silence. Gary's brain has now formulated an idea that meshes a dirty carburetor and a super-duper cleaning machine. Brilliant he decides. Just brilliant.

"Jo, you heard what she said right? It took off all the hard, baked on crust. You can see the evidence right here," Gary said holding up the pie pan.

"I see where you're goin' Gar, but I'm not so sure…"

"A little industrial strength grease buster and those high-pressure water jets. Press the heavy-duty button and my carb will be clean as a whistle."

Jo takes a swig of beer and is subtly bouncing her head in contemplation. That takes two seconds.

"How long will Doris be gone?"

"The rest of the morning. The wash cycle can't be too long."

"Let's do it."

"Oh baby. I can see a sparklingly clean Carter carb in my future! Jo, pick up the box and bring it over here."

Jo does so as Gary retrieves the instruction manual for the dishwasher from the counter drawer and starts reading. Jo places the box with the carb gently on the counter and starts to unload the dishwasher.

"Says here that the heavy-duty cycle will cut through just about everything… grease, baked on food, carb dirt…"

"Really?' Jo asks. "Lemme see."

"You just hurry up and finish unloading that thing. It says here that it'll take about 45 minutes to cycle through so let's get a move on. Doris will not be on the need-to-know list. Capeesh?"

"You think she'd have a problem with using her dishwasher for carb cleaning?"

"What she doesn't know won't hurt her. Almost done there?"

"Yep. All is ready for Sir Carter AFB. Come to mama…"

"Whoa there, Pocahontas. I'll do the honors."

"As you wish Kemosabe. Allow me to assist," Jo says as she slides out the upper rack.

Gary reaches into the box and carefully lifts out the sacred carb. Gently, he places it on the tray.

"Easy. Easy there, Gar'."

"Jo, it will be fine. It's been sittin' on top of 335 horsepower for all its life. I think it can handle anything this Maytag can dish out. Dish out? Hey, that's funny!"

"I'm in stitches," Jo says while sliding the tray back in. She starts to close the door. "See you in a bit, stay safe in there.' She opens the door again. "You be good now. Mama Jo will be right here." She closes the door briefly and opens it yet again. "Now when you…"

"Enough already!" Gary says. "Mr. Carter will be just fine." Why me? he lips to himself.

"Hey. I get to push the buttons and press start."

"Ok, fine. But first, go grab the bottle of green cleaner concentrate from the shop. It's on the…"

"I know. I know. I'll be right back."

Jo trots out to the garage leaving the door to the kitchen open.

"And bring the can of hand cleaner, too," Gary shouts after her.

"Got 'em both," Jo answers distantly. She fast walks back into the kitchen a bit out of breath.

"That's my workout for the day," she adds panting.

"Just open them up Marathon Mom. Let's fill the soap dispenser.

"Here ya go," Jo says taking off the cap of the Simple Green.

Gary reads the back of the bottle.

"One tablespoon per gallon of water. Whew. That's potent. I think one glug per tablespoon would be about right."

"How many glugs do we dispense?"

"Well, a few. I want it sparkling clean like the pie pan. And we only get one chance at this."

Gary opens the soap dispenser's lid and pours the green cleaner into the machine. The bottle makes its glugging noise six times.

"I think one would have sufficed. That's a lot of glugs."

"No. I think I got it about right."

"Suit yourself but I'll bet that dishwasher only used a gallon of water per cycle. Conservation you know. That's six loads worth of glugs," Jo explains.

"Yeah, whatever. The more the merrier, right?"

"Right by me," says Jo lofting her beer can and taking another swig.

"Now we'll throw in a scoop of the hand cleaner. It's got pumice in it to scrub those tight places."

"Sounds like a plan, Stan," Jo says as she takes a big wooden spoon from the utensil drawer, scoops out a dollop of hand cleaner and plops it into the dishwasher.

"There you go. Want fries with that?" Jo asks.

Gary gives Jo a smirk and with his index finger pointing the way, he continues to read the dishwasher instruction manual.

"Here ya go, Jo. 'For metal pans select hot water, heavy duty.' Got that Jo?"

"Hot water, check," Jo says as she turns the control

knob. "Heavy duty, check" she says pressing the button. "All systems are GO. Ready for final countdown."

Gary starts the countdown saying "Ten, nine, eight, seven, six (Jo has her finger above the start button now), five, four, three, two, one… fire!"

Jo looks quizzically at Gary saying "Fire? I don't think they say fire at Cape Kennedy."

"Just push the damn button,"

Jo does that and nothing happens. Nothing, dead silence. They trade puzzled looks.

"What you do?" Gary asks.

"Me press start."

"It no start."

"Me see that. Wait second," says Jo leaning her ear to the machine. "I think I hear something ominous sounding."

Gary glances at the panel display for some indication of what's happening.

"There! That light reads 'run'."

Jo starts running for the door yelling "She's gonna blow!"

"Come back here you chicken," Gary insists. "It's on and running. It's just so quiet that we didn't hear it fire up."

"You say run. I run. I ask no questions."

"Can we continue this in normal language?"

"Sure, but I'll cost you another beer."

"That will get you to ten o'clock."

"I need pretzels."

"In the pantry. So, I guess we're set for the next hour. We'll come back later and see how clean we got it."

"It? You refer to Sir Carter as 'it'?"

"You got 'it' for brains. So, in the meantime, we'll take off its… er, Sir Carter's intake manifold."

"I still think a fender would do."

"The only fender I want to hear about is Jimi Hendrix's guitar. To the garage!"

"Purple haze is in my brain."

"Ah, so that's what happened? Come on."

Gary puts his arm around Jo's shoulder, and they walk to the garage confident in their plan but unaware of what is happening inside the dishwasher.

CHAPTER NINETEEN

In the garage, Gary and Jo are under the hood pondering the intake manifold while listening to the Hendrix station on Sirius. They have an array of socket wrenches within reach on the workbench as they try to determine the proper size to remove it. The manifold has most likely never been removed and with fifty years' worth of static use, it has frozen itself to the engine block and doesn't particularly want to oblige a separation. They drench the bolt heads in Liquid Wrench and tap on them to set up a little vibration to help it along. They've been at it an hour already and a bead of sweat rolls down Gary's cheek.

"Gee wilikers these bolts are tight. We need to give the loose juice more time to work. Tap it again. We need to convince it that being tight ain't right."

Jo taps the bolt head a few times.

"That wasn't in time with the music. Get with the ambiance here, will ya?"

Jo puts the socket wrench to the bolt and tries to turn it to no avail.

"Still won't budge," Jo laments. "Let's give it more time to think over the consequences of not being on the same page with Gary and Jo."

"I'm hot. Let's get a cold one," Gary says.

"Ain't even lunchtime yet. You changin' your ways? Comin' over to the dark side?"

"Yep. With a Guinness. That dark enough for ya?"

"I like the way it bubbles backwards. Ya know if that carb comes clean, there's a whole lotta parts to do. We can give that Maytag a real workout," Jo says.

"For all the good money I paid for it, it better work. And only $25 a month on their finance plan. Doris wanted something special, and she got it."

"Married to you, she earned it."

"That's the tire callin' the fan belt black. And you're an Angelina Jolie I suppose?"

"She ain't got nothin' on me. I gots all the right junk, in all the right places."

"I'll have Fred confirm that."

As they continue to trade jabs, a scent of pine waifs into the garage. Among the other odors of oil, grease and loose juice, the pine scent has elbowed them out and risen to the top of olfactory detection. Jo crinkles her nose sniffing the air.

"Gary, do you smell what I'm smelling? Something… green?"

"Green? What do you mean green?"

"I dunno," Jo replies. "It's clean smelling. Sorta like that stuff we threw in the dishwasher."

"Hmmm. Maybe we ought to check on the carb."

Jo glances at the door to the kitchen and sees bubbles pushing out of the gap at the bottom.

"Gary, your kitchen is foaming."

"What? Foaming?"

Gary looks over to the kitchen door and his jaw drops.

"O M G!" stammers Gary.

###

Doris and Maggie have finished grocery shopping and are unloading the car. Each carrying two bags, they enter the front door since the garage entry has been blocked by the GTO and all the tools.

"I hope Gary and Jo have straightened things up in the kitchen. I spent two hours yesterday cleaning it from floor to ceiling and I asked him… make that *told* him to keep it that way," Doris says.

"We've only been gone two hours. What could he do?" Maggie replies rhetorically.

Doris pushes open the kitchen door with her foot and a three-foot-high wall of pine-scented bubbles cascades out.

"Let me rephrase that," Maggie quips.

"Wa. Wa. What is happening here? My kitchen is full of bubbles!"

"And they smell very green," Maggie adds.

"Why's my kitchen full of bubbles!" Doris screams. "GARY!"

Almost simultaneously, Gary and Jo open the door to the kitchen from the garage and there too a wall of bubbles pours out into the garage.

"I think you may have gone a bit heavy on the green stuff," remarks Jo.

"Ya think?"

Above the sea of bubbles that span the entire kitchen, Gary sees Doris on the opposite side just as she yells his name.

"Oh, hi dear. Home so soon?" Gary sheepishly asks.

"Jesus mini, Gary! What have you done to my kitchen? What's with all these bubbles?"

"I was cleaning the carburetor in the dishwasher and must have put in too much soap. The pine scent is a bit refreshing though, isn't it?"

133

"Gary, how are we… *you*… going to get rid of these bubbles? Everything is covered and I just cleaned it!"

"Well, I'll have to get back to you on that."

"Gary this really takes the cake! You gave me your word. What was it… scouts honor?"

"He had his fingers crossed on his other hand," Jo chimed in and regretted it the moment it left her mouth. Doris threw her 'the look.'

"I'm sorry Dor'. I didn't think this would happen."

"Hmmm. 'Didn't think' is what your problem is...has always been Gary," Doris says.

They start to slowly wade through the bubbles trying not to run into anything hidden in the mire. Suddenly Doris loses her balance, slips and disappears. A moment later, she reappears with her head full of bubbles and making a spitting sound. She wipes the mess from her face.

"You ok dear?" Gary asks.

"Yeah, I'm ok, but you are not!"

"I tried to tell him," Jo remarks.

"Two peas in a pod if you ask me. Gary, please explain… out with it!"

"You remember how you said that your dirty pan got so clean after you put it in the dishwasher? So, I figured…"

"You figured?" Doris interrupted. "I can hardly wait for this one."

"He thunk it up hisself," Jo nodded.

"I figured that I could do the same thing with my carb. Make it spic and span like the pie pan. I must have put in too much Simple Green."

"Really? That stuff is concentrated. One capful per gallon. How much did you use?"

"Six glugs," Jo injected.

"What's a glug?"

"When you tip it over and it glugs out... glug, glug, glug sounds. I told him to stop because six was too many."

"One would have sufficed. What am I saying? *None* would have sufficed and not in my dishwasher."

"Look, Dor', what's done is done. I'm really, really sorry. We'll clean it up better than ever."

"Oh, Gary. What am I to do with you? But you're right. What's done is done, but how do we get rid of these bubbles?"

"Simethicone!" Jo proffers. "That's what's in those gas pills for your stomach."

"Yet another brilliant idea from Dr. Maytag," Doris says. "A wet vac is the only way. We can't wait for it to dissolve. That'll take all day."

"Jo, get mine from the garage. We'll start at the door and suck our way in."

"Let's get debubbled before we all turn green," Doris says.

"Still love me, Dor?"

"I'll get back to *you* on that."

An hour later they got the bubbles sucked up and wiped down the kitchen. They are sitting around the island having a snack and drinking beers.

"It still smells green in here. Probably will for days. Open a window for some fresh air," Doris commands.

"I love the smell of green power in the morning!" Jo says.

"That was a great war movie... if there is such a thing," Gary replies.

"So?" asks Doris.

"So what?"

"So, what about the carb. Did it get clean?"

"Gee, I forgot all about it! Let's take a look" answers Gary.

Gary opens the dishwasher door and gently removes a now shiny, clean carburetor. Everyone is aghast at how good it looks.

"Wow!" exclaims Jo. "It looks brand new. I told you it was a great idea."

"The accomplice rats on herself... classic," adds Gary. "But I must say there's not a bit of grease or dirt anywhere!"

"Beauty is only skin deep. What about the innards?" Doris asks.

"That will be step two. Now that it's clean, I can rebuild it."

"Which should be left to the professionals," Jo says. "Put a screwdriver to that glorious carb and I'll never speak to you again!"

"Dor, quick. Get me a Phillips head."

"I think that's enough carburetor talk for today," Doris adds. "I'm mentally exhausted. You two are a handful sometimes."

Just then the dishwasher's door drops open by itself and everyone turns to look. It emits a long, loud burping sound.

"Simethicone!" Jo quips.

CHAPTER TWENTY

The trip to the car show had planted the seed of an idea in Gary's mind and it hadn't quite yet had time to germinate. Gary was continually trying to think up a way to get Doris aboard the Goat train, and late at night was no exception. Being of the age when his prostate started to rule the sleep cycle, Gary's nocturia would command him to get up to pee at 2:30. Gary would stumble into the master bath, lit with a dim nightlight, and do his business more often than not hitting the target. Another stumble back to the bed and under the covers, most of which Doris had pulled to her side. A tug or two elicited a mumbled complaint from her, something about her being cold, but eventually things quieted down. That is except for Gary's racing mind which invariably dwelled on the GTO.

Those early morning thoughts ran the gamut from tires to tune ups. Take the exhaust headers for example. He envisioned just how he would free them from the engine block in the tear down cycle. Spray 'em with liquid wrench, let 'em soak for a few hours, tap them once in a while to allow the stuff to penetrate and then crank on them with a long-handled socket wrench, hoping not to break the bolt. Hmm, he thought, maybe there are better ideas on the web.

After running through a few of these scenarios, it

was now 3:30 a.m., and he needed to get back to sleep. But as fate would have it, a brilliant idea popped into his head. The seed had sprouted! He'd take Doris to the local fire company's annual barbeque event just a few miles down the road scheduled for this coming weekend. It just happened to be right next to the big antique car dealer. She loved barbeque more than anything and this plot would surely get him into her good graces. And, by the way, they'd take a few minutes to walk through the dealer's vast showroom housed in an old shopping mall. Perhaps nostalgia would soften her adamant stand to dump the Goat. Well, it wouldn't hurt to try. Satisfied that the plan was a good one, he went back to counting sheep.

The next morning despite the intermittent sleep, Gary dragged himself out of bed before Doris awoke, bounced off the hallway walls on the way to the kitchen, and started to brew her favorite cup of java. After a few minutes, the wonderful aroma permeated not only the kitchen but crept down the hallway and into the bedroom. One wouldn't think that this aroma therapy would have a caffeine kick, but apparently a few molecules triggered her senses enough to arouse her from a deep slumber. With one eye open, she reached for Gary, found his side vacant and took a deep breath. Ahhh, that smells so good. She intuitively wondered what Gary was up to and what he wanted.

"Ah, good morning sweet cheeks," said Gary as Doris shuffled into the kitchen while knotting her bathrobe. "Have some coffee?"

"How could I not?" she replied as she rubbed the sleep from her eyes. "Why are you up so early? Didn't you get any more shut eye after you got up to go pee?"

"Of course, of course. I hope you slept well."

"Fine until I smelled the coffee. You know how to perk a girl up."

"Here's your share," said Gary handing her a cup. "The Half and Half is on the counter."

Doris shakily poured the creamer, took a tentative sip and relished the first hit. Gary might be a handful at times she thought, but this was nice. She took a bigger sip.

"So, I've learned that there is a big barbeque competition today down Morgantown way. Want to go?"

The one-two punch, right from the get-go. And so early in the morning before her brain had engaged. She pulled up a stool and sat at the counter. Coffee, barbeque… he's pushing my buttons.

"Ahhh, yeah. I could suck on some ribs, but later maybe. I need a croissant first. A competition you say?"

"Yeah, all the big grillers will be there. You know, the ones with the giant trailers emblazoned with their team names and logos. World class stuff."

Doris's stomach started to growl. Smoked ribs, pulled pork and that oh-so-tender brisket. It had been a long time since she'd had some of that, the price of meat being what it was. Yeah, she'd go regardless of what she thought Gary might have up his sleeve.

"OK, let me get my head together and get my, and our, chores done."

Gary didn't divulge his ulterior motive of course, thinking that it would be appropriate to suggest a stroll around the car mall *after* the barbeque event. How could she refuse after chowing down on those exquisite ribs? After all, marriage is a sharing arrangement, isn't it?

###

139

By lunchtime, all the chores had been done, and they headed down Route 10 to the barbeque event. Gary was right. All the famous grillers were there and by invitation only. The trailers were lined up and the teams were actively preparing their meats for judging which had just started. Runners with Styrofoam trays of superbly barbequed chicken thighs and drumsticks, the first of the four required meats, were walking quickly to the big tent where the judges were seated six to a table. There was a subtle feeling of excitement in the air along with the savory smells of barbeque.

Gary parked the car far off the end of the row of trailers. There didn't seem to be many, or any, other people in attendance, only the grillers.

"Where is everyone?" Doris asked. "For all these teams, you'd think there'd be hundreds of folks here."

"Let's find out," said Gary as they strolled through the smokey rows. They caught the attention of one couple who were just slicing up some perfect looking ribs. Their trailer proclaimed "Pork-o-tonic."

"Hi, there," said Gary. "Nice looking ribs."

"Thanks," replied the man. "Appearance is one of the judging criteria. I hope they like the taste. That's where the big points are."

"Yeah, sounds logical. By the way, I don't see any people like us snatching up all these ribs. What's with that?"

"We can't sell our meats to the public… state vending regulations. This competition is just for us. A share of the $15000 in prize money."

"Oh baby," said Gary. "That's a lot of dough. The way your ribs smell, I think you got a shot."

"We hope so," replied the woman who was prepping

the container with a bed of kale. "We've been at this since six a.m. just like everyone else here. We came in third last year in ribs, eighth overall."

Gary's and Doris's stomachs growled in unison, and they looked pensively at each other.

"So, we can't buy any food here?" asked Doris dejectedly.

"Nope. Them's the rules, laws actually," replied the man. "But come back about 1:30 or so."

"Why then?" asked Gary.

"Well, we can't sell it, and we can't eat it all. We're either going to give it away or throw it out," the man said.

The woman pointed to a small counter with plastic bags and gloves.

"The judging will be over by then, so come back and take what you want… free of course."

Gary and Doris were flabbergasted, and their stomachs growled even louder.

"Ohhhhh, baby!" exclaimed Gary. "We'll be here, right on the dot!"

"Ok see you then, but for now, we gotta get these ribs on their way to the judges and start workin' on the brisket."

At the mention of brisket, Doris's mouth started to water so much she had to lick her lips, and she could almost taste it from the savory smell wafting up from the smokey grill. Seeing the look on Doris's face, the woman cut two small slices from the brisket and handed them to Gary and Doris.

"Here," she said. "Maybe this will tide you over."

Doris bit off half of her portion, closed her eyes and concentrated on the flavor.

"Oh… my… god," she whispered. "This is absolutely

delectable. I've never tasted anything close to being this good."

"Thanks," said the man. "I hope the judges feel the same way."

"Tastes like first place to me!" said Gary. "Good luck and see you a bit later."

They ambled through the rows of busy teams and bid their time until the formal competition was over. Promptly at 1:30, they were back at the Pork-o-tonic site stuffing plastic bags with four different meats. They also stopped by last year's champion at the suggestion of one of the judges they had met earlier. There they got even more brisket. They decided that when they got home, they'd invite the gang over for their own taste testing.

"There's a cooler in the trunk. Let's put the meat in there and take a few minutes to check out the car mall," said Gary. "I put some ice packs in there too. Along with the beer."

"Did you now?" asked Doris. "Surprise, surprise."

"Gotta keep those Yuenglings cold."

"So, pop me one while you're at it. Looks like your little plan is working out."

"Plan? I ain't got no plan," questioned Gary with his fingers crossed. "Here's your beer. Let's get to the car mall."

Turning on his heel and grabbing Doris's free hand, they made for the car mall and found there to be a car show in the parking lot outside complete with an oldies rock 'n roll band. Ribs, beer and rock 'n roll thought Gary. Does it get any better than this? Well, maybe.

After taking in the music and perusing the display of show cars, they went inside to see long aisles and rooms filled with dozens of cars running the gamut from decrepit Model Ts to 1950s hot rods to sleek Mercedes AMGs. Gary was sure that he'd find a Goat or two in the mix and pulled Doris along.

"You in a hurry, Gary? I want to see that '55 Chevy over there. My dad had one."

"No, no hurry, just a lot to take in."

They checked out the Chevy and a few others along the way but hadn't found any GTOs yet. Gary was starting to get a little worried that they might not currently have one but as they turned a corner to walk down the next aisle, there it was. A '66 GTO, completely restored, and showing off its deep Montero Red paint and black interior. Gary was stunned and Doris took note.

"Aha," said Doris. "I see what you're up to. It's a beautiful GTO but look at the price tag on it. $25,000!"

"Man, prices have really gone through the roof. That car was $3200 new. Inflation I guess, not to mention the big demand for classic cars these days. There are a lot of retired guys who invested in cars rather than CDs."

"Jesus mini, Gary. I appreciate the ribs, the beer, and the music but I'm sorry. This Goat project cannot proceed. We've been over this a hundred times. We just can't afford it."

"Ok, ok. I guess you're right. While we're here, I'll talk to one of the salesmen and leave my number with info on my Goat. Maybe he'll have a lead."

"Good. Then we'll head home and invite the neighbors for all this barbeque. I still love you by the way."

"Love you to, Dor," said Gary. The wheels in his mind had already started to work on another plan but forces unknown to Gary were about to come to his aid.

CHAPTER TWENTY-ONE

After the first attempts and eventual success of starting the GTO, the ignition key was left inserted into its receptacle on the wood-veneered dashboard just to the right of the steering wheel. Gary wanted to get a duplicate made but for now the safest place to prevent losing it was right there in the dash. Dangling from the lone key was a common beaded chain which held a worn brown leather fob darkened by innumerable grasps of hands now lost to the ages. The ancient oils and subtle odors of the leather were now being refreshed by the new hands of Gary and his garage crew, an occurrence not lost on the keen olfactory sense of the one passive team member… Nicky. Having the run of the house and the garage through a large dog door, Nicky came and went at will. His arrival in the garage was uniformly greeted by a pat on the head, a gentle rubbing of his ears, or if Jo was there, a bit of kibble she kept for him in the back pocket of her bib overalls.

For safety's sake, after the greetings and pettings, Nicky was told to go sit on his comforter under the table which held the TV. For this bedding, Doris had selected an old bedspread from the master bedroom on which Nicky had spent countless nights sleeping curled up at the foot of the mattress. Two adults and a hundred fifteen-pound dog made for tight sleeping positions and Gary often complained that that queen size was definitely too small. Of course, the bedspread held familiar human and canine odors despite an occasional airing out or a less frequent washing. So the comforter became the perfect cushion for Nicky to curl up on as he kept company with the ersatz mechanics.

When the crew left the garage to get a bite of lunch in the kitchen, Nicky was free to nose around the car and explore for new sights and scents without being told to 'go lie down'. Following Jo's scent, uniquely highlighted by a morning splash of Estee Lauder, Nicky ambled up to the open driver's door and peered in, nose probing. Here he picked up another more interesting scent… food! While Jo was sitting in the seat working on fastening a loose wire, a bit of kibble had worked its way out of her back pocket and onto the carpet between the front seats. Nicky jumped up onto the driver's seat and had no trouble following the scent but had to stretch his tongue to get at the morsel lying way under the passenger seat. The kibble was dispatched in two chomps and Nicky turned his attention to other matters. His eye caught a glimmer off the key chain and his nose followed with a probing of the old leather scent. Hmmm, he probably thought that at one time it was edible, but it now held the subtle scent of his master. A quick lick verified that it would be a pleasant accoutrement to his lair, and he gently grabbed the fob in his teeth and pulled out the key with it.

What a prize! With the key chain dangling from his mouth, he looked up and around to see if anyone had noticed his burglary. Seeing no one, he had to step over onto the passenger seat to turn around because the steering wheel was in the way of his large body. He jumped out of the door and made a quick trot around the car and onto his comforter. Two complete circles were needed to condition the bedding, and he plopped down with the key chain still hanging from his muzzle. His instinct was to bury the prize, so he placed the key chain in a loose fold of the bedspread and with a few taps of his paw, the treasure was hidden from any curious eyes. And who would suspect a loyal and lovable friend of such a mischievous deed?

CHAPTER TWENTY-TWO

Gary was in a sour mood as he dictated the wording of another for sale ad to Jo. He had forestalled the inevitable day by artfully dodging Doris's demands to sell the Goat. His offers of a romantic candlelit dinner or a spontaneous trip to the creamery only met with a dead-panned scour. Her heels were dug in deeply and nothing Gary could do would change her mind.

Jo typed in his less-than-positive ad copy and offered suggestions to make the ad even less appealing. But how could they demean a car that meant the world to them? Any car guy that saw the ad would read between the lines. They knew what lurked under the hood and under the rust, dents and dirt. They took the requisite pictures under dim lighting and refused to clean off the dust that had accumulated. But place the ad they did which was necessarily corroborated by Doris. Game on.

Lo and behold, no less than a dozen requests for more information came in in the first two days. These missives were slowly responded to and only in terse, fragmented wording which perhaps gave the impression that the seller was a nut case. Mission accomplished thought Jo knowing that Gary *was* a nut case albeit an increasingly shrewd one.

After warding off most the inquiries, there remained one persistent gentleman from a nearby town who unfortunately knew a friend of a friend of Jo's. This meant that they had to give the guy the courtesy of a quick look at the car lest Jo's reputation become besmirched. He'd be there Saturday at the crack of noon.

Gary and Jo both refused coffee that Saturday morning and put on their game faces. They traded tired-eyed facial expressions and stopped with the friendly jabs and retorts. Doris caught on to the act and warned both of them to cut the crap and sell the damn car. Chagrined, they put their tails between their legs and shuffled out into the garage to await their fate.

The guy was ten minutes early and jauntily said that his motto was 'if you're not early, you're late.' Looking around the car, he seemed to like what he saw through the camouflage. He wasn't stupid and he caught on to the charade but said nothing. In his mind, it was a buy only if the engine started.

"So can we fire it up?" asked the buyer.

"Sure, why not?" mumbled Gary. "Jo, get the jumper cables and hook 'em up to the extra battery. We'll need all the amps we can muster to get that finicky starter to engage."

"It's been an on again, off again thingy," chimed in Jo. "I'm thinking it's something more serious way down in the flywheel."

With a suspicious knowing nod, the man said "Ok, well, we'll have to see I guess."

Jo fumbled with the cables and accidentally on purpose touched the live ends together creating a brilliant spark.

"Wow, that's a lot of current," she exclaimed. "I better be more careful."

Playing the fool was generally Gary's realm but she

opted in like a pro. All thumbs and little brains were the call of the day. Gary was duly impressed but her bib overalls and do rag didn't quite fit with the numbskull routine. He hoped the guy didn't notice the inconsistency. He did but remained silent.

"Ok now Jo. I'll get in the car and crank her over. And spray a bunch of that starter fluid in the carb right away."

"Roger dodger," Jo replied.

"Ok, mister, here we go. I hope she starts for ya, I mean me."

Gary reached to turn the key but found it missing.

"Hey, Jo. Where's the key? I thought we left it in the ignition?"

"We did, absolutely did. No reason to take it out as we discussed. It's gotta be there."

"Well, it ain't here," said Gary as he started to scan the dashboard, floor and seats. "It ain't nowhere."

"Don't you have a spare key?" asked the man with a hint of suspicion in his voice.

"Ahhh, no. I was going to get one but haven't gotten around to it. My bad… as they say."

"May I suggest that we cross the wires behind the ignition switch," he proffered.

"Just like on TV!" Jo said to which Gary gave a 'what are you thinking' look of displeasure.

"I've never done that," said Gary. "I wouldn't even know how."

"Might I try?" said the man. "I spent a month in the slammer for doing the same thing many years ago."

"Oh, well then, have at it," Gary said.

Gary exited the car and the man sat on the door sill as he reached under the dashboard and started to fiddle with the wires. Gary and Jo traded questioning looks and shrugs.

"Are these wires hot?" came the question from under the dash.

"My pleasure," responded Jo as she touched the positive cable to the battery terminal.

The blue flash that erupted from the car's interior took everyone by surprise not the least of whom was the man. A plume of acrid, white smoke rolled up over the dash and drifted out the open door. The man exited the car while rubbing his head.

"I meant it to be a simple question, my dear. Not a command to engage the cable! You have played the dimwit long enough, but now I'm thinking that there is an ulterior motive behind the ruse. You both are cut from the same cloth, and I think that I will no longer play along. You can take your car here and shove it up…"

"Whoa, whoa. Let's not get all excited," injected Gary. "We need to sell this car, sir. I apologize for our incompetence. Won't you reconsider?"

"Methinks not."

Just then Doris enters the garage with a tray of cookies for Gary, Jo and the guest buyer.

"Why hello there. I'm Gary's wife Doris and you're here to buy the GTO. Congratulations!"

"My dear, I beg your forgiveness but I must demure on my ostensible interest in this car. It seems as though your spouse and his accomplice here have conspired to negate my purchase. And they have succeeded. And you seem to be such a wonderful person to have chosen this… well, need I say more?"

The man nods, grabs a warm cookie and does an about face and strides out the garage door.

The dead silence lasted only a few moments before the anger rose in Doris's face.

"JESUS MINI, GARY! What in god's name have you done now? That was supposed to be a qualified buyer and there he goes in a huff. Speak to me!"

"We couldn't find the key to the Goat. It wasn't in the ignition. It was his idea to hot start it by crossing the wires under the dash. I'm guiltless!"

"Another word you can't spell. Jo, what did you do?"

"Me? He asked for juice, and I gave him juice. A hundred amps worth. I couldn't see what he was doing under there. His fault, not mine, not ours."

Nicky smelled the cookies and got up from his bedding and ambled over. He stood in front of Doris and slowly wagged his tail while keeping a fixed stare at the plate.

"Nick, I'll give you only one and no more. You're lucky I ran out of chocolate chips, or you'd be getting none," Doris admonished. "Now sit." He sat. "Good boy!"

Simmering down a bit she turned her attention to Gary and Jo.

"You guys are going to be the death of me yet. Oh well, here, have a cookie. So, what happened to the key?"

"No idea. It was there last time we worked on the car. Honest to God."

"Well look for it and find it before the next buyer comes. No excuses. I want this car gone."

"Ok, ok. It'll turn up somewhere. Maybe we'll have to buy a new ignition once the smoke clears."

"Nicky, you come with me, and we'll let these two clowns to their hunting. But I want to get your bedding and hang it on the line to air out."

Doris walked over to the table and reached under for the comforter. When she pulled it out, she heard a faint jingle and then the car key dropped to her feet. They all gazed at the key and simultaneously shouted "Nicky!"

Nicky cocked his head, licked his muzzle and gave a brief wag of his tail hoping to get another cookie.

CHAPTER TWENTY-THREE

The days ticked by with Gary spending all his free time in the garage preparing the GTO for resale much to his chagrin. To lift his mood, he'd put some tunes on while he tinkered away. Gary's taste in music didn't extend too far beyond twelve bar blues. He'd learned a few chords on the guitar Doris had bought him for Christmas early on, but he preferred listening to practicing.

As newlyweds, they both enjoyed dancing, especially at the 'retro' sock hops and rock 'n roll dance halls. Being a bit of a ham and showman, Gary liked to dress the part as well. Before it thinned out, he combed his hair in a pompadour complete with a 'duck's ass' finish in the back. He'd wear a tight white T-shirt, jeans with a black belt and, get this, he sprang for a pair of blue suede shoes as a tribute to Carl Perkins. Of course, Doris was not to be out done and poured herself into undersized jeans and a slightly revealing halter top. The black, high heeled 'do me' boots, as she referred to them, completed her ensemble. The pair of them was not to be outdone and they were quite popular back in the day.

More recently, Gary laughingly suggested they dig out the old threads and let the good times roll but Doris didn't bite as her figure was a bit fuller and she no longer wore skin-tight clothes. Gary occasionally threatened to one day step into those blue suede shoes and tear up the dance floor once again to which Doris suggested he set up a subsequent appointment with his chiropractor… just in case. Today, they are sitting around the kitchen island munching on granola and reading the newspaper's weekend section.

"Dor, there's a rock 'n roll revival concert and dance at the Hamburg Field House next Friday night. Are you game?" Gary asked.

"Me? Are you? You're the one always bellyaching about your back… or your shoulder… or your 'insert body part here'," Doris answered while making quote signs with her fingers.

"That's what ibuprofen is for. I'll worry about my threshold of pain later."

"Last time we danced rock 'n roll you were twenty years younger. Your threshold of pain then was quite low. It's most likely subterranean now."

"Hey, I can deal with the pain if you can deal with the whining. It'll be fun. We'll get the whole gang to go… Jo, Fred, Maggie, Burt… we'll have a blast. Ya dig?"

"Hmmm… maybe. I suppose I'll have to endure the associated lingo… ya dig, cool, daddio… ad nauseum."

"All youse chicks can put on some fine threads, A-Go-Go style, and get hip!"

"Why me?" she muttered.

Gary, now excited with a new 'mission', turns on the CD player and pops in a 'Greatest Rock 'n Roll Hits' disc and cranks up the volume. The first song out of the box is Little Richard's 'Tutti Fruitti,' and Gary grabs Doris' hand to join him dancing. She rolls her eyes but rises to the occasion and in a few moments the chemistry between them is back. They cut the rug for the entire song and are breathless by the end.

"I, I need to… catch my breath" Doris pants.

"Me too. That was fun and hey, we still got it!" Gary adds.

"You shoulda put on a slower song first. Little Richard is a bit wild to start with."

"Yeah, we'll have to practice and build up some stamina. We can't have the rest of the crew out-dance us. Let's give them a call and sign 'em up. We won't take no for an answer" Gary insists.

"Ok, I guess I'm in. We do need a night out," Doris said and sat down to finish eating.

"Fan-freakin'-tastic! You call 'em up and I'll go dig out my old threads. They're probably still in a box somewhere around here. And I almost forgot… I still have my old blue suede shoes!"

Doris coughed up a spoonful of her granola.

"You ok, dear? Was it something I said?" Gary asked.

"No, no. I'm fine. You can look around, but it's been a long time. Maybe we should just go in regular clothes. Why bother dressing up?" she proffered in trying to divert the issue of old clothes and blue shoes.

"The ad said that there are prizes for best dancers and best dressers. We can win both!"

"Well, we'll see. Hey, you promised to mow the lawn and it's getting late," Doris said trying again to change the subject.

"Yeah, ok. I'm on it. We'll rock later."

Doris had suddenly lost her appetite for granola or anything else for that matter and thought maybe she should have looked a little more closely at Gary's boxed stuff before she tossed them. While Gary hit the lawn, she went to the basement closet and rummaged through the few boxes that remained of Gary's. It didn't take long before she realized that his old 'threads' were gone along with his cherished blue suede shoes. Why, she thought, was I so stupid, so selfish. It really wouldn't have been a big deal to keep his stuff as there was plenty of room. It just needed some reorganizing. But how was she going to break the news to Gary. He'd be heartbroken. He hasn't been this excited about something for quite a while and now she'll be busting his bubble. 'Think, Doris', she said to herself. 'There must be a way to fix this mess, but how?'

It had been a while since she and Maggie dumped the boxes at Goodwill but maybe the shoes were still there. She dialed Maggie.

"Maggie, it's me. I'm going to be in hot water with Gary if I don't recover some of his stuff that we threw out the other day."

"We? I asked you if it would be alright with Gary. What happened?"

"He read that a rock 'n roll show was coming up nearby and got excited about going. You're both invited by the way. But the problem is I think that I tossed his old blue suede shoes along with all the other junk. He cherished those shoes and wants to wear them to this song and dance show. If I don't find them, he won't speak to me for a week."

"There are worse fates. Hey, hold on a second. While we were loading, I was checking out one box and, at the bottom, I saw a pair of blue shoes. That must have been the ones you're looking for."

"Oh, Maggie, that's wonderful! We're going to drive over to Goodwill right now before they get sold off to some-one with size eleven feet and a strange taste in footwear."

"Let me finish with these cookies I'm baking. Ten minutes."

###

Doris and Maggie parked the car in the rear of the Goodwill building near the drop off door. A man and a woman were helping another donor unload boxes of clothes, toys and household goods from her car.

"Excuse me" Doris said to the woman who seemed to be overseeing the donation area. "We have a problem. We dropped off some boxes of clothing the other day and one of the boxes had items of sedimental, er.., sentimental value to my husband. Is there any way we can look through this area to see if we can find it?"

"Gee, I don't know honey. There must be a hundred boxes here and obviously we are very busy sorting and cleaning. You'll be in the way of progress," the lady re-marked.

"It would mean a lot to my husband… to me."

"As long as you stay out of the way and put things back in place, I'll let you do it. But please be careful. You never know what's in some of these boxes. People donate the strangest stuff."

"Oh, thank you so much. We'll do as you wish."

A hundred boxes was a low estimate. There were easily one fifty or two hundred and to make the search even more daunting, most were typical tan cardboard and Gary's would be the needle in the haystack. But into the fray they plunged, one box at a time. Maggie would lift a box to a nearby table, and Doris would open it and check for the shoes and finding nothing, sealed it back up for Maggie to restack it. After about fifteen minutes, Maggie's back was aching, so they switched jobs. Back and forth they continued with this ridiculous tag team scheme for three hours all to no avail. They plopped themselves on a donated loveseat and wiped their sweating brows, exhausted and hungry.

"All that work and nothing to show," Doris said.

"I'm feeling muscles I didn't know I had," Maggie lamented.

"Me too. Sorry to drag you into this Maggie. You're a good friend."

"Hey, we gals gotta stick together.'

The manager of the Goodwill store ambled over having heard of their plight. He looked at the big pile of boxes and then at the two tired women moaning on the loveseat.

"You two are diligent workers. If you ever need a job sorting clothing, give me a call," he jested.

"Thanks, but I think our sorting days are over as of day one," Doris said.

"So, what are you looking for exactly? You obviously didn't find it."

"Blue suede shoes. An heirloom of my husband's that I accidentally donated here. Three hours of backbreaking work and nothing."

"Size eleven?" the manager asked.

"Yeah, size eleven. How did you guess that?"

"No guess. They're out in the retail store. You couldn't miss them on the men's shoes rack. They stand out like a sore thumb. Ain't too many blue dress shoes come in here. First ones actually."

"You mean to tell us that the shoes are out in the store, and we didn't have to spend all afternoon busting our butts looking through all these boxes?"

"In a word… yes. I suppose they got processed and labeled yesterday. In doing my rounds, I only saw them on the rack today. They looked so good that I picked 'em up but I take size nine."

"So, they're still on the rack as we speak?" questioned Maggie.

"Yeah, unless someone has bought them. But I don't think blue suede shoes are in high demand."

"They are in my family," Doris said. "Maggie, let's go!"

The manager pointed to the doorway leading to the retail store and told them to find Jimmy, who was in charge of the men's department. With a surge of adrenaline, Doris and Maggie bolted through the door and into the store. They stopped briefly to scan for the men's department, and seeing it, they hurried over. Jimmy was sorting some shirts and hanging them by size. Doris and Maggie approached him and asked him about the blue suede shoes. He said that the shoes had just been put on the shoe rack last evening so they should still be there. He stopped what he was doing and led them to the shoe area.

"The shoes are all sorted by size. I distinctly remember them. Blue suede kinda sticks out from the browns and blacks. That pair was right here, second row and the end of the rack. But I don't see 'em now," he remarked.

"The store just opened a half hour ago so where could they have gone?" Maggie asked.

"Maggie, there are only a few customers here right now. You take the right side of the store and approach them to ask about the shoes and I'll take the left side," Doris ordered.

Frantically they tracked down each customer, but no one had taken the shoes. As they stood bewildered in the middle of the store, Doris noticed a woman wearing a hot pink scarf at the checkout line.

"Maggie, did you question that lady with the pink scarf?" Doris asked.

"Never saw her. I surmise that you didn't either."

"Miss! Oh Miss!" Doris yelled as she bolted to the front of the store.

"I'm sorry to bother you but did you by chance happen to grab a pair of blue shoes?" Doris asked the lady.

"Why yes I did and here they are," the lady responded while lifting the shoes from her cart. "I picked them out for my husband, size eleven, and in nice condition. He'll love them for his birthday tomorrow. And a bargain for only ten bucks."

"Well, ya see. Those shoes actually belonged to *my* husband, and I inadvertently donated them to Goodwill the other day as I was cleaning out a closet. Would it be too much to ask if I could have them back?"

"I think not. I desperately need something for his birthday tomorrow. Sorry, no can do."

"Please, please, pretty please," begged Doris. "My Gary will be heartbroken. He's owned them for twenty years and as you can see by their condition, only wears them infrequently. How about I give you twenty bucks for them?"

"Tempting, but I've fallen in love with them since they'd make my George very happy."

Another customer, a flashy-dressed guy, was in line waiting to check out and overheard the animated conversation.

"Sweet shoes, honey. If you're sellin', I'm buyin'. Thirty bucks!" he offered.

"What?" Doris exclaimed. "You can't do that. They're for me. You butt out."

"Thirty dollars is even more tempting," the lady said holding up the shoes and looking them over.

"Oh hell, forty bucks!" Doris fumed as she peeled some cash from her wallet.

"Fifty," the guy said. "They'd be two hundred new and I want them bad now that I've seen how popular they are."

"Jesus mini! You people! Have you no decency? If it wasn't for my mistake, we wouldn't be standing here bidding on my own husband's shoes!"

"You made the bed," the guy grumbled "so you gotta sleep in it."

Maggie had caught up and was listening nearby. She dug into her wallet and pulled out a crisp C note.

"One hundred," Maggie said slamming the hundred-dollar bill on the counter.

"Wow, another bidder! Anyone else in the store want in?" the lady exclaimed.

"I'm with her," Maggie stated. "One hundred, take it or leave it."

"But, but…' the guy grumbled.

"Sold!" the lady said and quickly snatched the bill from the counter and stuffed it in her purse. "George won't miss what he doesn't know. Here's your shoes. Enjoy."

The lady then handed Doris the shoes, and she hugged them to her chest.

"Thanks Maggie. You saved me. That forty was all I had."

"You can square up with me later. I'm just glad we found 'em."

"You and me both. Especially me. Now all I must do is repack them in a box and put 'em back in the closet for Gary to rediscover."

"Let's get back before Gary starts snooping around. He'll never know this happened. Today's your lucky day Doris!"

"But let's get a margarita first. I need a while to chill."

"Sammy's here we come!"

CHAPTER TWENTY-FOUR

Gary had gotten the lawnmower to start after a dozen pulls on the cord and a hefty shot of starting ether. 'Son of a gun, I aggravated my rotator cuff', he thought as he rubbed his shoulder. A new lawnmower was way, way down on his list of replacement tools so dealing with the hard start was a weekly affair unless his prayers for a drought came through, in which case he'd get a reprieve long enough for his shoulder to ease up. He enjoyed the mowing which provided an hour's respite from the myriad of problems that weighed on his mind with the GTO issue right on top. He inserted the ear buds under the earmuffs, tuned in some blues and started pushing. He finished in forty-five minutes just as Jo showed up.

"Gary, I saw you mowin' and need to borrow some gas. I just ran out and need to finish my back yard."

"Where's Fred? Ain't that his job?"

"I have him painting a bedroom. His allergies are bad, and he'd rather not mow."

"What a wuss. Ok, here's the gas can. Take it and bring it back whenever. I won't need it until next week. Oh, so are you guys game for a rock'n roll dance party next Saturday night?"

"I guess. Where at?"

"Hamburg Field House, seven o'clock. I'm gonna wear my blue suede shoes!"

"You have blue suede shoes? Who does that?"

"Had 'em since Doris and I were young boppers. I think they're in a box somewhere. Let me put this mower away and we'll go look."

"I gotta see this. My lawn can wait."

Gary rolls the mower to its designated spot in the garage, throws his work gloves on the bench and leads Jo through the kitchen and down to the basement. Everything there is tidied up and the closet hasn't looked this organized in years. Gary is bewildered.

"Wow, Doris must have spent hours down here cleaning this up. It looks fantastic. So neat and organized and all the boxes are labeled. Mine should have 'Gary's stuff' written in marker on the end."

"Really? How creative."

"Weisenheimer. I think I remember it being a cardboard box with red lettering so that should help us find it."

"I see mostly cardboard, some white, here's some blue ones. None with red lettering."

"I know it's gotta be here. Hell, it's been in this closet for what... twenty years? It didn't up and walk away!"

"Maybe it grew legs and feet, and it strolled out wearing those blue suede shoes!"

"Stroll is the operative word. With my feet in 'em, those shoes can do The Stroll... one of my favorite dances. But, hey, me no see um the box."

"Ditto for me. There must be three dozen boxes in here, maybe it's behind something."

"Or maybe she repacked it in another box. I guess we must open all of 'em to see what's inside."

A half hour later they had opened all the boxes but much to Gary's lament, none contained the shoes.

163

"Dang, this was the last box and nothing there either. Maybe she decided to put them somewhere less musty."

"Well, Gary, I hear my mower calling. Just wait for Doris to get home. She's sure to know where they are."

"Yeah, you're right. Thanks for helping."

"Thanks for the gas so we're even. I just had a bad thought. I hope she didn't throw them out."

"No way, never. She knows how much those blue suedes mean to me… to us. Nah, she packed 'em away somewhere, you'll see. Speaking of the devil, I think I hear some footsteps in the kitchen. Up we go!"

Meanwhile, Doris and Maggie had arrived home from the detour to Sammy's after downing only one margarita and counting backwards from ten for Janey. It took two tries for Doris, so Maggie got handed the keys. Doris donned Gary's black 'What's cookin' good lookin' apron because hers was in the wash, and they started in on Maggie's bumbleberry pie recipe. Flour dusted most of the front of the apron and nearby, Maggie was ladling out the sour cream for the special dough recipe that was the foundation of a bumbleberry pie creation. Blending the ingredients for the dough, Doris asked Maggie to wash the fruit and preheat the oven to 425 degrees.

"Ain't that too hot for a pie," Maggie asked.

"That just gives the crust a head start for a few minutes. I'll reduce the heat to 375 for the rest of the baking."

"I like this recipe already. Blueberries, blackberries, raspberries, and a can of tart cherries all bumbled together. Who'd a thought? I can't wait to take a bite! I think this will be a winner, Doris."

"Wait 'til you taste the crust. That sour cream is the secret ingredient... so don't tell anyone!"

"But where'd you get the recipe?"

"On the internet."

"Good. No one else knows."

"Right. So keep it between us and maybe Jo. No one else!"

The basement door opened and into the kitchen walked Gary and Jo.

"Gary... and Jo," Doris stammered somewhat surprised. "Weren't you mowing the back yard?"

"Finished up a while ago. I told Jo about the dance party and they're in. I decided to look for my blue suedes and Jo was helping me. You did a great job organizing the cellar closet by the way."

"Uh..thanks. Maggie helped a lot."

"Leave me out of this conversation please," Maggie interjected knowing what was coming.

"So, Dor, I couldn't find the box with my old blue suede shoes in it. We looked through all of them and came up empty. Did you come across them when you were cleaning up down there?"

"Uh, uh, I didn't see them," Doris proffered barely skirting the truth.

"But I know they were in that jumbled mess somewhere. They were in a cardboard box with red lettering if I remember correctly along with some clothes. Are you sure?"

"I, uh, didn't see them," Doris reiterated as she tried to focus on kneading the dough and refraining from looking Gary in the eye.

"Would you have moved the box to somewhere else? Maybe up in our bedroom closet? Gary asked.

"Well, you know Doris, I have to be leaving now," Maggie interjected. "Got work to do at home with Burt. You and Gary have fun now."

"I smell a rat," Jo stated as she sniffed the air.

Everyone glanced at each other and then at Doris who was still very intently kneading, head down and focused.

"Ok, what's going on here" Gary inquired with a concerned tone to his voice. "Dor… Dor!"

"Oh Gary, I'm so sorry."

"Ok, sorry for what?"

"Sorry for throwing out your shoes. You left it all up to me when you went to play golf."

"The old blue suede ones. The one's with decades of sedimental legacy?!"

"That's sentimental but, uh… yes."

Gary ceremoniously grabbed his chest and took a seat on a kitchen stool. The color had drained from his face as he pondered what she had revealed.

"My… my shoes. Why did you do that?

"It was an accident. I didn't mean to. I was tired, in a hurry to finish and wasn't thinking right."

"Sorta like accidentally buying a GTO," Jo remembered.

"Exactly! See! What comes around, goes around!" Gary said. "Now it's up to you to find 'em. I hope they didn't make the garbage pickup the other day."

"No, we took them to Goodwill," Maggie said.,

"So, you're an accomplice to this crime of the century, Maggie?"

"An unwitting one. I did try to warn her about throwing out your stuff."

"Perhaps I'll get a little reprieve on selling the GTO," proffered Gary.

"That colossal mistake hardly equates with an old pair of shoes," Doris said.

"My blue suedes are not just an old pair of shoes. They have gobs of sedimental value," Gary added.

"*Sent*imental," Doris corrected.

"That's what I said. Sedimental. Well, whatever. You go find my shoes while I tinker with the Goat."

"Actually, Gary, we won't have to go far. They're back. We went back to Goodwill and luckily fortune smiled upon us. We found them but had to pay some lady a hundred bucks to hand them over. She had picked them out for her husband's birthday. Maggie saved the day by outbidding some other dude."

"Outbidding? Gee that sounds familiar," said Jo.

"Touche'," said Doris. "But I righted the wrong. Gary, you still must do the same."

"I know, I know. The GTO has got to go. Thanks for getting my shoes back. I'll keep working on selling the Goat," said Gary hoping that he'd get as lucky as Doris.

CHAPTER TWENTY-FIVE

Gary also had the ad to sell the GTO running on craigslist and Facebook marketplace and was getting a lot of tire kickers. Another guy was coming the next morning and in talking with him, Gary thought he was a serious buyer. He'd restored his own GTO and was looking for another project. He had cash in hand and seemed to share Gary's enthusiasm for the car. Plus, there was Doris's mandate to not aggravate prospective buyers after that last misadventure. She'd also warned Nicky to keep his muzzle out of the car.

The thought of the Goat being handed off to someone else had Gary in a funk. It appears only a miracle could keep the GTO in Gary's garage. Gary wasn't one to pray for material things, but he made an exception for the Goat.

That evening, Gary, Jo, and Burt were hanging in the garage and were tidying up the Goat for its probable sale. The esteemed Sir Carter was gently mounted back on the engine making an incongruous sight. It gleamed as new atop the grimy engine and seemed, at least to Gary, to plead a mournful goodbye. With a half-inch socket in hand, Jo deftly secured the carb to the manifold as Gary and Burt stood solemnly by.

"Well, that does it. The Carter is firmly in place," said Jo.

"Yeah, thanks Jo. You did good," commented Gary.

"I feel like we're putting flowers on a casket," added Burt. "I wish I could have come up with an idea to avoid this."

"I guess it just wasn't meant to be. It's another entry on my list of goof ups."

"Hey, Gar', you know I started you down this path," said Jo. "The blame is on me."

"It took two to tango. It was a fantastic idea and still is in my book. And we had fun while it lasted."

"I don't know. I have a funny feeling about this whole affair," said Burt.

"The last funny feeling you had was in your nether regions when Bonnie was feeding you that pizza!" joked Jo.

That comment broke the icy pall. They all belly-laughed and gave Jo high-fives.

"Speaking of pizza," said Gary. "I'm hungry… and thirsty. Let's crack some beers and order one. Half mushrooms and half pepperoni. Does that work for you guys?"

"Why the hell not?! No sense bemoaning our fate. Onward to the next adventure!" said Burt.

With that, Gary dialed for a pizza and Jo got some cold ones from the fridge. St. Pauli Girls were handed out and the fraulein on the cardboard beer carton was cut out and pinned up with the others above the workbench. They took a couple of swigs and set back to work on reassembling the parts of the Goat that were previously removed. The hub cap was snapped back on the wheel which held the once flat tire that Jo had patched. She was somewhat proud that it still held air. Burt was contorted in the back seat area cleaning out some debris before replacing the seat bottom that he'd cleaned and coated with Armor All. Darn if it didn't look almost new. Heck, it should, he thought since back seats seldom get much use except sometimes in the carnal sense. In the cleaning, he'd already found two quarters and a ballpoint pen. Hmmm, interesting, he thought. It had a local address printed on the side. He stuck it in his shirt pocket thinking finders keepers and went ahead cleaning out the rest of the lost junk.

"Hey Gary. Look what I found," Burt said holding up a woman's necklace."

"Cute," said Gary. "That'll go good with your halter top."

"I might have to buy a pink one. This necklace has rose quartz stones so I gotta do matchy matchy."

"You better or the fashion police will be hot on your trail."

"Hey, we can do a date!" said Jo. "There's a gay bar downtown and you'd be my arm candy."

"Sorry Jo. I've never gotten that drunk or stoned," Burt answered.

"Come on Burt. I've always wanted to check out that bar but didn't want to get hit on."

"Burt, just hang it on the rearview mirror," Gary interjected. "Maybe one of the wives will want it… or not."

Burt reached forward and after clasping it back together, slung it on the mirror. Then he squirmed out of the car and rubbed his aching back. He'd put the seat in later.

"I don't remember back seats being that hard to get out of."

"That's why they make four door cars. I'll find you a '66 Bonneville sedan at the auction," Jo proffered.

"Whoa there. I think we're done with auctions for now. At least until our sentences are commuted."

"Spoil sport! Where's your spirit of misadventure?"

"I'll reconsider after the beer and pizza which by the way is heading up the driveway as we speak."

Gary sprang for the pizza and tipped the delivery guy who unfortunately wasn't Bonnie nor Brenda. As they sat around eating the pizza, Doris and Maggie showed up also entering from the driveway.

"So, Gary, no hottie girls delivering today?" quipped Doris.

"We thought Jo needed a fix, so we asked for a guy."

"He was pretty cute," Jo added. "But I'm still in hot water with Fred, so I had to pass."

"It looks like you guys have got the car pretty much back together. Doris told me that a guy is coming tomorrow to buy it," said Maggie.

"Yeah, looks that way," said Gary dejectedly.

Doris looked at her forlorn husband and felt a pang of guilt course through her body. But she had made up her mind and wasn't about to change it. The cost of the car, not to mention its restoration, had put their finances in a bind which couldn't be allowed to persist. She was sorry to have hurt Gary's feelings, but he'd get over it... sooner or later.

"By the way, Burt found a necklace which is hanging from the rearview mirror. Maybe you gals might want it."

Maggie walked over, reached into the GTO and retrieved the necklace. She examined it as she swirled it through her fingers and sensed a somewhat vague thought developing in the recesses of her mind. Something about a necklace but she couldn't remember the details.

"Pretty stones and gold plated. And look, here on the back of the clasp are some initials. D.I.R." said Maggie.

"Close to yours, Doris. Except for the R," Jo said.

"They were my initials until I married Dr. Strangelove here."

Doris walked over to Maggie.

"Maggie, may I see that a minute?" asked Doris.

As she looked over the necklace, she realized exactly what she held in her hands.

"Gary!!!! It's mine! It's my necklace from the accident! How… how can that be??"

"Oh my god, do you know what this means? Can it be true? I must have bought dad's old car," Gary said. "I can't believe it."

"I'd forgotten that I lost it when we had the accident. But it is… it's mine!"

"And one more thing," said Burt taking the ballpoint pen out of his pocket. "I found this pen in the car too. It reads 'Hiway Drive-in.'"

"It's your dad's car, Gary. No doubt about it," added Jo.

Doris was just about jumping out of her skin and hugging Maggie in excitement. Maggie returned the hug and whispered in her ear.

"My thoughts exactly, Maggie. Gary, let's keep the car," said Doris.

"Wwwwhat? Did you say I can keep the car?" asked a flabbergasted Gary.

"No, I said let *us* keep the car. It will be our joint project with a little help from our friends here. Evidently the stars were aligned to bring this car back into our lives. I realize that now. We'll find a way to afford it… somehow."

"Ohh, baby! Dor, you are fantastic. This is a day we'll never forget."

"So, let's celebrate! Beers for everyone!" exclaimed Jo as she opened the fridge and distributed cold bottles to everyone.

"Here's to Doris. My wonderful wife!" proclaimed Gary as he lofted his bottle.

"Here, here!" they all shouted in unison.

Gary leaned back against the Goat, shook his head in disbelief and smiled.

Later that evening after everyone had left, Gary replaced the back seat bottom that Burt had carefully cleaned and given a light rub down with protectant. That Burt, he thought, does nice work and it only cost me a few oatmeal cookies. He plopped himself down on the seat to make sure it was snapped in place, then sat back and smiled as he looked around the interior still amazed that the Goat was really his. Who would have ever thought that he'd have a Goat in his garage? He closed his eyes for a few moments and silently gave thanks to the greater power that in spite of his misdeeds and colossal goof ups, was always there to heal and forgive. For that he was grateful.

The opening of the kitchen door aroused him from his brief meditation, and Doris entered with two bottles of St. Pauli Girl. She shook a blond curl from her eye and walked over to the side of the GTO.

"Thought you might be thirsty," she said.

"You thought right," Gary responded as he reached out for the frosty bottle.

"Room for two in there?"

"Absolutely but you'll have to come around to the other side because the driver's door here is jammed."

She nodded okay and walked around the front of the car stepping over the small parts that had been removed from the headlight bezel. As she rounded the right front, she put her hand on the loose fender and lost her balance

173

as it moved. She had to quickly step sideways to recover and as she did, Gary cautioned.

"Careful there, honey. Watch out for the m…

Snap!

"Owww! Gary!"

"…mouse trap. Which I guess you found."

"Jesus mini. It got my big toe! Lucky for you it hit the leather of my shoe, but it still stung a bit."

Gary slid over on the seat and looked out the open rear window.

"Sorry 'bout that. Hey, weren't you a Mouseketeer when you were a kid? I guess I caught a trophy mouse!"

"Wasn't I once your trophy wife?"

"You still are. Hop in."

Doris shook the mousetrap from her toe, opened the passenger door and pushing the front bucket seat out of the way, stepped into the Goat. As she sat next to Gary, he grabbed her foot and massaged her toe.

"Does that feel better?" he asked.

"Yeah, thanks," she said taking a swig from the bottle.

"So many years ago that we were sitting in this very same car on our first date," Gary mused.

"Well, it took a while, but you finally got me in the back seat."

"Yeah. Think I'll get lucky?"

"Depends. Were you hoping to get lucky back then?"

"Of course, but then we had the accident."

"I guess we'll never know what would have happened."

"So, what about now?" Gary asked.

"Hmm, after all you put me through lately you're lucky to be breathing. But I forgive you. Guess what I'm gonna make you?"

Gary shrugged.

"A cross-stitched plaque that reads 'Gary's Garage.'"

"Sounds so manly. I'm sure I'll love it. And I love you."

"I think your pheromones just kicked in. You might get lucky after all."

"I'll drink to that," Gary replied as they clinked their bottles, took a quick sip and then a longer kiss.

The End

Or is it the beginning?

www.ingramcontent.com/pod-product-compliance
Lightning Source LLC
Chambersburg PA
CBHW071118100726
47908CB00008B/2416